Roadkill

Roadkill

Helen Whistberry

Other Books by the Author

Standalone Titles:

The Melody of Trees: 10 Tales from the Forest

The Tail of Nightshade

Once Upon a Wave of Witches (with Eli Belt)

When Your Heart is a Broken Thing

The Final Voyage of Avery Mothmere

The Jim Malhaven Mysteries series:

The Weird Sisters

The Avenging Angel

The Ghostly Groom

This one is for me

Contents

Content Warnings

This is a work of horror fiction and as such contains images and themes that may be disturbing to some readers.

Content warning for dead and mutilated animals, body horror, gore, death including implied child death, mentions of homophobia and transphobia

Vulture

The winds aloft are violent tonight. The sky has a peculiar green glow which dissolves into a vomitous pink along the horizon, and lightning from a distant storm flashes from cloud to cloud but never once strikes the ground. My wings catch and ride the updrafts as easily as ever, but there is a heaviness to the air which oppresses my mind and weighs my body down. I'm not superstitious—few of my kind are by our very nature—but even so, my thoughts are full of foreboding and vague memories of whispered stories within our committee gatherings, tales that speak of eldritch events and visions of a Day of Reckoning.

Fighting against the downward drag, I fly higher, circling and circling, head cocked, one eye on the earth, one on the sky. I'm big and fierce enough that not many bother me up here, but I've been wary since an eagle caught me off guard. Nyx saved me. Drove the thing off with her sharp beak and talons. She was a good mate. Loyal and true. I mourn her still and hold her spirit warm within me.

I spy a deer carcass. Always chancy when you're close to a human path. It's how I lost Nyx. But it looks to be that rare kill no other has discovered yet. To have it all to myself and not squabble and shove and fight for a place at the feast is an unusual treat, so I land by the head as it's farthest from the hazard zone. I think plucking a juicy eyeball will be the best place to start, but it blinks at me. Startles me into jumping back, wings aflutter. Could have sworn it was dead. We have an instinct for these things. A waiting game then. I prefer my meat thoroughly deceased. Less trouble that way.

The deer catches me watching as I settle into my vigil and I swear it winks at me. Licks its bloodied lips with a long pink tongue. It staggers up to its feet, delicious guts and luscious organ meat falling heavily from a gash in its belly. The skin is abraded from its side, and the shining whiteness of bone flashes.

"How are you alive?" I ask.

"Don't think I am," it answers, head lowered to the ground as it sniffs at its own entrails.

I am struck with shivering. It speaks flatly, and I see no rise and fall from breath. Can't hear the steady thrum of a heartbeat. A dead thing that walks and talks. Surely there's a less unsettling meal elsewhere. A human path is always rich with the slain. I move along and find a raccoon down the way, nearly decapitated. Drag it farther into the grassy verge. It rewards me by biting my beak with a vicious snarl. Doesn't hurt, but it's still a hell of a thing.

"What's happened?" it hisses.

"Guess you were hit?"

"Remember the lights. Blinding. Stupid humans. Am I dead?"

"I thought so."

"I think so too," it says, holding onto its head with both front paws to keep the flopping thing from falling off completely.

A squirrel chatters up to us. It's flattened but somehow still finds the energy and balance to stagger about. An orange tomcat, fat as a tick and crawling with maggots, swishes its tail as a jackdaw and crow land in awkward somersaults, made clumsy by their broken wings but full of squawks and jabbering. The disemboweled deer ambles down the highway to join a gathering crowd.

I am a creature inured to death. You might say it is my stock-in-trade, but even I find this all a bit much. Dead things should stay dead, unmoving and well-behaved. These creatures are anything but.

I hear a crash through the woods behind us. A black-furred bear. It flops about like every bone in its body is shattered to pieces, but it moves with a jerky determination.

"COMRADES!" it roars. "OUR TIME HAS COME!" It sees me, grins, wide-mouthed and excessively toothy. "You have also known sorrow from the tyranny of humans. Join us, friend."

A claw swipes across my throat and breaks my neck. I collapse to the ground, black out for a moment before I come to and stand, head slumping to one side so I'm forced to view the world askew, but one soon gets used to anything, I find.

I am one of them now. We march down the center of the human path. Others join us, crawling out from shallow graves of mud and old leaves. Many are no more than a loose pile of bone and gristle yet somehow have the strength to move. A sorry-looking crew—grotesque and disfigured. Yet, in my slanted view, noble, filled with grandeur and a common single-minded purpose.

The first lights appear. The humans screech to a stop, slewing broadside across the path. The men in the box get out to stare. A fatal mistake. There is little left of them in a short time except a few tufts of hair and bones strewn about. Other humans are more wary. They remain inside their boxes, peering out disbelievingly at us.

No matter. Mice can crawl through the smallest gaps and their sharp teeth send our victims scrambling out within our reach.

The dead's appetite is never satisfied. Our ever-growing army spreads out to the neighboring nests where humans roost in the dark. No barrier can withstand our determined assault for long. Other humans arrive in boxes with twirling lights and screeching whines. They knock a few of us aside, fire metal seeds, but the dead cannot be killed and we are many. I enjoy the screams. Retribution is a most pleasant melody.

Brethren continue to pour in to bolster our numbers. Those of us who can fly scout in every direction and report back. East, west, north, south, armies are on the move. Human blood without measure is being spilled. We will reclaim this land as ours and the human paths will grow wild once more. Return to a place of quiet and safety. And those creatures alike to us yet still among the living will know peace at last. Our gift to them before we lay our weary bones down and become one with the soil unto which all must return soon or late.

Deer

Heads up. Ears twitch. Snort and puff. A warning. White tails flash. Scatter.

Run!

Twin goes one way. Escapes.

I go another. Mistake.

S c r e e c h

An agony of time and pain.

Sharp beak. Vulture. It startles. Retreats.

I'm not dead I am dead I'm not dead I am

Stagger up. Things drop to the ground. Things that shouldn't. Don't like the sound they make.

S q u e l c h

Vulture speaks. "How are you alive?"

"Don't think I am." The voice is not mine. Or is it?

Bend down to sniff at the things that dropped to the ground. They smell of my scent and not of my scent. A sharp tang. An unpleasant spice.

Vulture wanders away. Wants nothing to do with me. I want nothing to do with myself.

No choice.

Walk along. Things drag and tangle. Trip and fall to my knees. Bones shatter. Makes no difference.

This is what we feared so much. A lifetime of *panic* and *run* and *hide* and *keep still so very very still...*

Death is not so different after all except there is no fear. Feel its absence like an ache. A hollow sound.

Other weird creatures gather ahead. I miss my herd so I join this one instead.

There is talk. I am distracted by the dragging things. The crowd is excited. They are leaving. I follow and trip again.

"Allow me, comrade."

A bear. Scoops up the dragging things in its paws, rips them away. I feel the parting but no pain. Walking is easier. Bow my head in thanks. The bear oozes away like a slug on the ground. Another broken thing, yet kind in its way.

Don't know where to go. Follow my new herd. They are stopping humans. Killing.

Hang back. Watch and listen. *Wonder.*

Orders are given. The herd scatters. I follow the nearest. Raccoons, chattering and chirping. They ignore me.

Deep grass. Take a few bites but it has no taste now. Pity.

Raccoons are busy. Tearing and biting. Humans scream. Never knew they could. Sounds like a fox in heat.

Small human runs my way. Upright and furless and wide-eyed. Red-stained cheek.

We stare. Brown eyes to blue. It whimpers.

A fever comes. Lift my front legs to *STRIKE* and *STAMP* and *MAIM* and *KILL* and...

"No, Sister."

Soft voice. Familiar. Alive and warm and breathing.

"Come away with me," it says.

My fever breaks.

My old herd gathers. They sniff at my scent.

Heads up. Ears twitch. Snort and puff. A warning. White tails flash. Scatter.

Run!

I am now the thing they fear.

Raccoon

Chiby got it in the neck. Two-wheeler. Told him not to fool around in the road. He was trying to impress a dame, naturally. Head's barely hanging on. Dame ran off. Typical.

Mizn and me leg it down the way. There's a bridge over a shallow creek ripe with crawlers. Nighttime's best. Not many men about and the crawlers are sluggish and sleepy, easy to catch.

Don't like the looks of the sky. Stormy. Flashes light the road as we go but the rain never comes. I'm hot and itchy. Take a load off to scratch my back against the bridge post. Never see the damn thing coming. No lights, no warning—just lights out for me.

I come to, surprised I'm not dead. Check myself over. Back feels funny. Kinda crunchy and loose. Spot Mizn in the road. Poor sap. Flat as a beaver's tail. Coulda knocked me flat myself when he sat up and waved me over.

"What happened to you?" he asks.

"Whattaya mean what happened to me? How're you even talking? You're squashed like a bug!"

"Well, you're all bent in two. Ain't you got no spine?"

I realize then what's up—back's broken. I ain't in no better shape than Mizn. We both oughta be dead. It's a peculiar feeling, I can tell ya.

"What's it all about, Terbs?" he asks.

"Dunno. We're stiffs, I guess, but we ain't exactly. Maybe this is what happens after you die."

"Ain't never seen no corpses walking around conversing before."

"True, but something's in the air tonight. Look at the sky. Ain't never seen nothing like it."

"Whatta we do?"

That's a puzzler. Chiby and Mizn always look to me to take charge since I'm first born of our litter. Gets tiresome to tell the truth. Why I always gotta be the one to come up with a plan? Besides, I thought once you was dead, you wouldn't have to worry about such things no more.

"Can you walk?" I ask.

He peels himself up off the road and totters along like a leaf blowing in the wind. Don't seem possible but somehow he's doing it.

"I got an idea we should go check on Chiby," I say. "Maybe he ain't exactly dead neither."

We waddle back down the road. Must be a peculiar sight as neither of us is in great shape but we soon find out we ain't alone.

There's a commotion up ahead. Lots of chumps gathering. They look to be in about as sorry a shape as us except for a black vulture who's hopping around giving everyone the stink eye. What's he so high and mighty about?

There's Chiby, holding his head up with both paws. He waves at us but has to catch his melon when it tries to take a dive. "Hiya, brothers! Looks like you had a bad night too."

I gotta agree. "Not the best. What gives with the crowd?"

"Dunno. Something's brewing, but nobody knows what."

There's a crash behind us. Black bear breaks out of the woods. He's a big brute and normally we'd scatter, but seeing as we're part of the dearly departed and the bear is stumbling around like he ate too many rotten apples, we just watch to see what happens next.

The bear exchanges a few words with the snooty vulture, then kills it with a casual flick of his paw. The vulture don't seem to mind. It shakes it off and follows the bear but now it's got a crooked neck and ain't so far above it all. One of us.

We get some rousing patter from the bear who's flanked by a grey wolf with its back half missing and a red fox that's more bones than fur.

"Who died and left them in charge?" Chiby says with a hoot of laughter. He's always been a joker.

"Top of the heap, ain't they?" Mizn points out. "Guess death ain't much different than life. Still think they got the right to lord it over the rest of us 'cause they're bigger and meaner. Whattaya think about what he's saying, Terbs? This stuff about the day of man being over?"

"Bout time," I say. "They been taking us out left and right as long as any can remember. Our turn."

I rub my paws in satisfaction. There's a feeling rising up in me I ain't never had before. A righteous anger. That's it, a righteous anger. Who do humans think they are anyway?

The crowd surges out onto the road. We follow and stand around gawking at the first attack. On the second, we join in. At a signal from the bear, we break into groups to start rousting men out of their dens. My brothers and I pick up a few more of our kind along the way to form our own gang.

"I know a place," I say. "They like to take potshots at you if you wander through the yard. Let's start with them!"

No argument from the crew. I notice a young doe what's dropped most of her guts following us. Seems kind of lost but we ain't got time to babysit.

I lead the way through the hole in the fence. It ain't even like we gotta be quiet 'cause there's a helluva noise blaring out of the picture box they stay glued to. Chiby and I scout out the scene. Four big ones and two little. There's a dog chained in the yard but he barely lifts his head. I seen one of the big ones beating on him plenty. He won't bark and give warning and I don't blame him none.

Mizn is the skinniest of us, what with being flattened. He finds a loose screen and snakes his way in through an open window. Works on the knob of the back door until it swings in. Always was a clever son of a sow. We saunter inside. They ain't expecting us, that's for sure. Chiby and I tackle one of the big ones together. Chiby bites onto its arm. It tries to shake him off but only succeeds in throwing my brother's body to the ground. His teeth and head ain't letting go. I coulda laughed it was so comical, but I got my own part to play.

I vault myself over some of their stuff and grab the big one round the neck, biting deep into the vein throbbing there. Don't take long for it to bleed out. I carry Chiby's head back to his body so he can pull himself together best he can and turn to see what's next.

Three of the big ones and one little are laid out on the ground already, but I spy through a window a big and little sprinting away outside.

"Come on, fellas!" I rally the troops and we chase the big one and drag it down. The little one escapes but it won't get far. It's barely old enough to walk.

Our fur is slick with blood. I feel powerful and right and as satisfied as I ever felt in all my days. This is what we were made for. This is better than life.

I follow the little one's trail. That deer is there—the gutless wonder. She rears onto her hind legs with blood in her eye.

"Yeah," I cheer, "do it!" but a herd of live ones wanders up just then.

The dead doe looks embarrassed, like she's been caught out doing something she shouldn't oughta.

The herd catches the whiff of death from her and they turn tail and run. I look at the doe. The doe looks at me. The little human sits on the ground and wails.

"I'll take care of it," I say.

The doe hesitates, nods her head, turns away as I get to work.

Best night ever and it's just getting going.

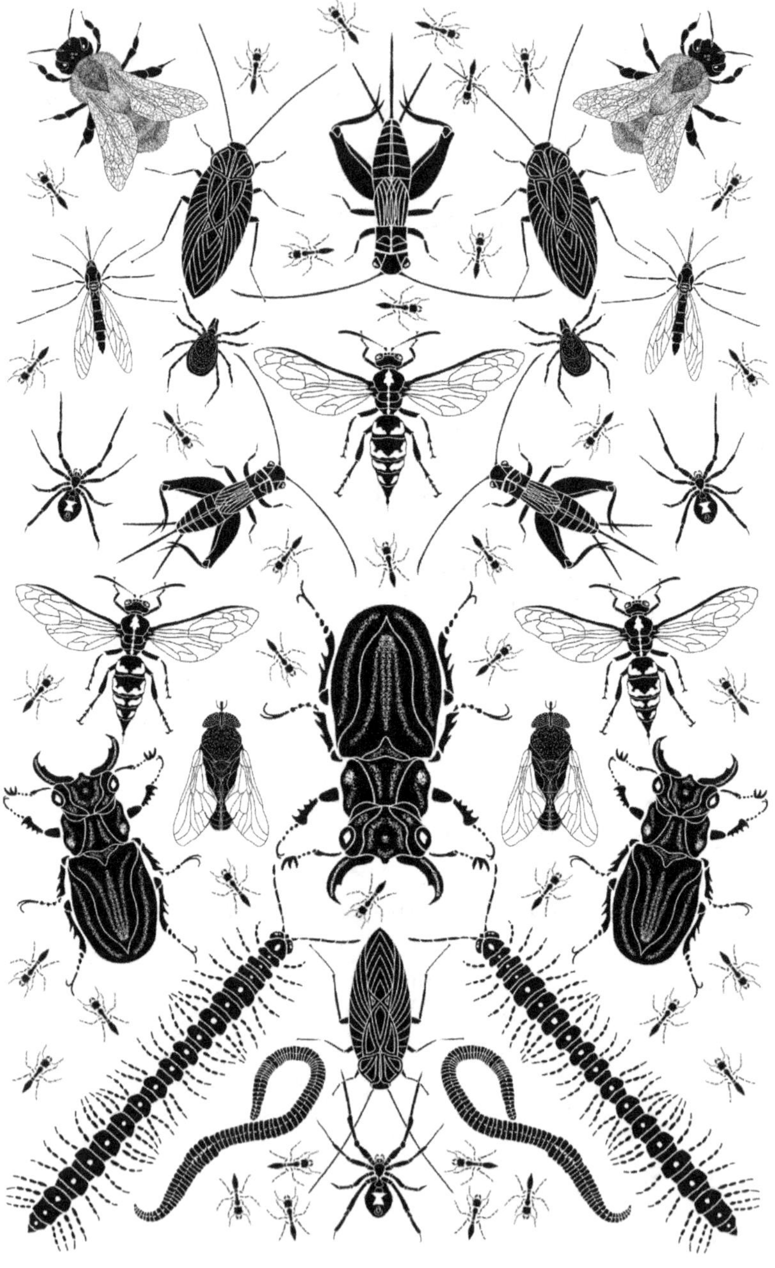

Insects

we are legion legion legion

the noise we make
an unholy din and hum and buzz
how lovely how lovely

crawl stalk fly flutter
wriggle bite sting creep

how many of us
splattered on glass
crushed under rubber

swept through
the burning death of the
infernal human machines

we are nothing nothing nothing
on our own

so feeble
so delicate
so easily crushed
or brushed away

but together
we are legion

Human: Lise

Most of the town is dead or dying as far as we know. We're making a last stand at the old Methodist church on the corner of Fifth and Main. It's been abandoned since the 90s when the congregation aged out and died off. The stained-glass windows are broken and boarded up. Doors are chained. It makes for a reasonable fortress against the larger creatures, but there's no sealing out the smaller ones, not without more supplies.

There's talk of making a run to Jayce's Hardware for insulating foam, duct tape, anything to stop up holes and cracks, but no one volunteers to give it a try. Only a block away, but it might as well be on the moon. No one who steps outside is gonna last more than a minute or two.

Daddy sits with the other men in the pews at the back. They clutch their shotguns and rifles, knuckles white from the grip they keep on them. It's like they can't give up faith in their weapons even though they've proven worthless against this relentless enemy. They're deep in the same arguments which circle round and round about what to do and get us nowhere.

The women moan and clutch their children to them—those who have managed to see them safe to this temporary shelter at least—while others sit in shock, empty-handed, barely aware of anything but the nightmares replaying in their heads.

Jenny and I have organized the older kids and teens into a loose circle around the pews. We're trying to make a game of stomping as many of the beetles and roaches, spiders and centipedes which form a constant parade from under doors and cracks where floor meets wall. You have to grind them to dust under your shoe or they keep moving.

We've scared up some fly swatters and rolled up old church bulletins to slap at the flying insects. There's not a one of us who's not bitten a dozen times already. Turns out poor Henry Brock was allergic to bees. Nothing we can do for him. Even in these few short hours, we've grown callous to death. Ignore it and move on. Try and keep as many of us alive as we can until rescue comes.

We're about evenly divided on whether help is on the way or not. Maybe it's the difference between who sees a glass half full and who sees it half empty. I've always been a pessimist myself. Why would our town be the only one under siege? I figure everywhere's got the same problems. Government'll come, some say but what would they do? Bomb us to hell most likely. That's their answer to any invasion, from without or within doesn't matter.

I don't speak aloud on it 'cause it won't help any, but I think this is the end. Been expecting some kind of apocalypse most of my life and this seems as good a one as any to go out on. Lord knows these creatures have plenty of reason to want revenge on us. Haven't I spent most of my life counting out the roadkill on the side of the road? Trying to identify it as we fly past in the car. Give it a last feeble dignity of at least a moment of recognition of what it was and that it once existed in the world. Not that my guilt and sympathy will save me from their wrath.

A new commotion starts up by the altar. Rats and mice have found a way in, tearing a hole beneath the wooden lectern big enough for others to follow. The heavy old bible resting there falls to the floor with a boom like the crash of thunder. Men rush forward, start blasting. The noise and stench of gunpowder are unbearable. The children wail. The critters keep coming. We are in hell, but I take comfort in the fact it won't last long.

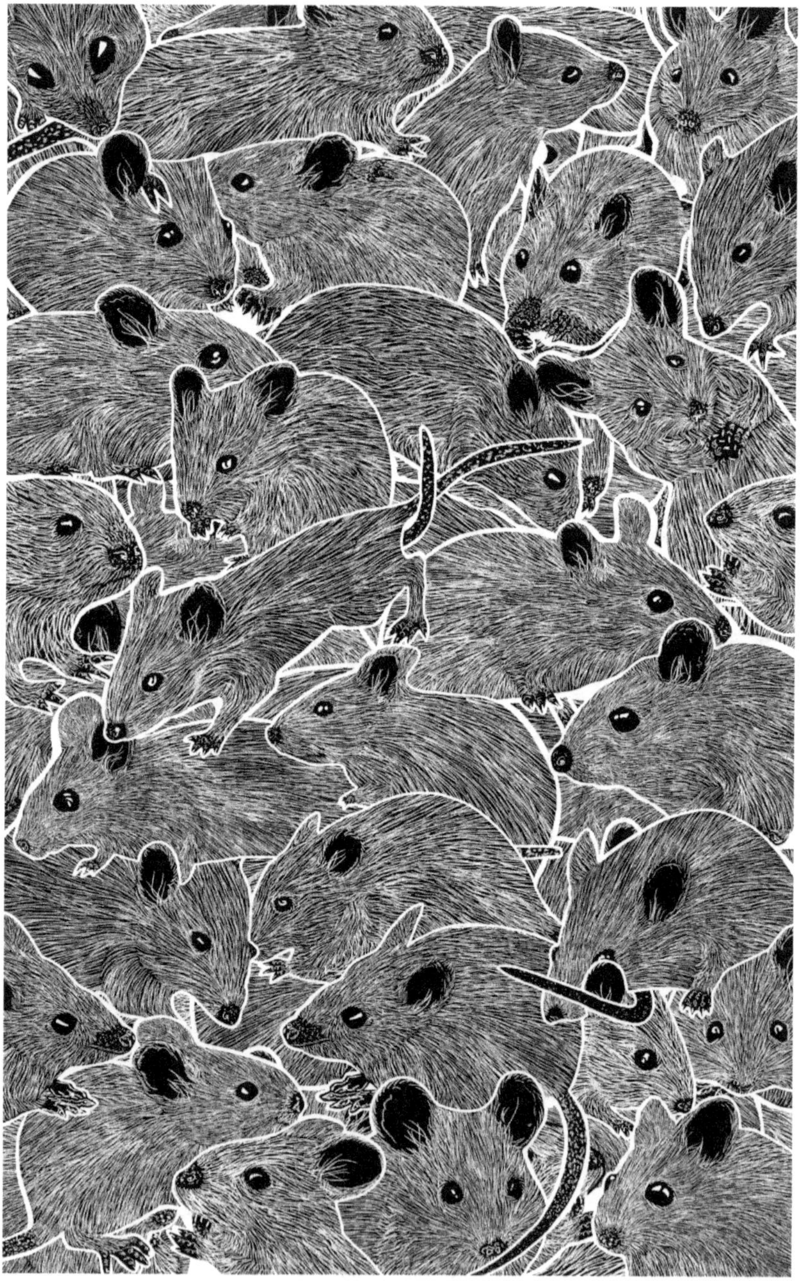

Mice

scurry

scurry

scurry

climb (hide) climb (hide) climb

s k i t t e r and s c a m p e r

cHeW

squeezetighttighttight

bite bite bite bite bite bite bite bite bite bite bite bite bite bite bite bite
bite bite bite bite bite bite bite bite bite bite bite bite bite bite bite bite
bite bite bite bite bite bite bite bite bite bite bite bite bite bite bite bite
bite bite bite bite bite bite bite bite bite bite bite bite bite bite bite bite
bite bite bite bite bite bite bite bite bite bite bite bite bite bite bite bite
bite bite bite bite bite bite bite bite bite bite bite bite bite bite bite bite
bite bite bite bite bite bite bite bite bite bite bite bite bite bite bite bite
bite bite bite bite bite bite bite bite bite bite bite bite bite bite bite bite
bite bite bite bite bite bite bite bite bite bite bite bite bite bite bite bite
bite bite bite bite bite bite bite bite bite bite bite bite

Bear

This is the moment I never dreamt of but understand I've been waiting for all my life. As I crawl from the ditch where the humans left me a shattered, jangling thing, the laws of nature no longer bind me. I answer to a different set of commandments now.

I sense there are bands of warriors forming far beyond my ken. Feel them deep within this shapeless husk of me though my eyes could never see so far. Fierce words echo inside my skull. *Fight... avenge... destroy...* the time of man will come to an end as is only right. This world will be ours again. But first, I must gather my own army.

Even in death, my nose is keen as I sniff the air. A gathering of the slaughtered is near. Except for one. One has a different scent. Has not yet crossed over. It is a mournful, lonely thing. I decide I will find it and put it out of its misery. One more soldier for the cause. The vulture's neck is fragile and breaks easily.

I've often thought myself a foolishly clumsy beast and now more so than ever. The difference is, I no longer care. I hold my head high as I'm able and the others look at me with awe and respect, even broken and bent as I am. They must feel the power surging within me. See the magnificent vision I hold in my mind as I roar out orders.

A grey wolf and a red fox volunteer as my lieutenants. Natural leaders, us three. They understand the mission right away and break off to organize the milling crowd, nipping and biting at those slow on the uptake, until our battalions are on the march.

We take the lead in demonstration of might and method in our first skirmishes. Our troops are quick to learn, eager to serve, mad with a desire for blood that any follower of mine will need this night. Once they see the way, the crowd scatters, each to deal out death in whatever fashion best suits their kind.

I watch them go, wishing I could accompany each one, be everywhere at once, witness every kill for myself, but I feel the glory of their merciless hunger resonating in the distant cries, the crunch of bone, the tang of iron the wilding winds waft my way. Though it may be hard won, our victory is never in doubt, for we have nothing left to fear and the humans have all too much.

What power do the living hold over the dead? None to compare with our combined might. At the thought, my soul roils with such delight that I must let it out. I roar and roar and roar again, adding to the din and chaos. And when I am bored with roaring, I shriek with laughter, and which of these sounds most terrifies my countless victims, I neither know nor care.

Possum Hare Heron

"If that bear doesn't shut the fuck up." The possum was a walking skeleton, but that didn't stop it from hissing to itself through its remaining teeth in disgust.

"What will you do?" a hoarse voice inquired.

The possum had seen many a weird sight already on this night of nights but this one ranked high. A hare's head without a body levitated before what once were the possum's eyes but now were only empty bone sockets in a cracked skull.

If it had the time or wit to think on it, it might have wondered how it could see at all, but it was busy deciphering what was before it: a hare's head (and head only) suspended by one long raggedy ear from the sharp beak of a heron. The bird was tall and stately except for its wings which trailed at unnatural angles along the ground, shedding blue-grey feathers as it stalked forward.

"What the fuck happened to you?"

The hare's head blinked its eyes, appearing to cogitate upon this question before answering the possum. "Rather rude, aren't you? But your kind often are, I've found. Obviously, I've met with something of an accident. Makes it challenging to get around but fortunately for me, my compatriot here," the hare twitched its nose and whiskers in a vain attempt to point at the bird, "found me and is assisting with my perambulations."

"The fuck you say."

"I'm not sure what you mean exactly. Could you elucidate?"

The possum stared in scorn and disbelief, but as it had no eyes nor muscle or skin to form the appropriate expression, the effect was somewhat diminished.

"Ah, I see I should speak more plainly for those less erudite than myself." The hare sniffed. It began to speak slowly and extremely loudly. "LOST... BODY. BIRD... HELP... WALK."

"Fuck this." The possum scraped itself away, bones making an indescribably unpleasant sound as they slid over rough pavement.

The hare was not the type to be so easily dismissed and urged the heron to follow. The bird, with its long strides, had no trouble keeping up even as the possum sped up its escape attempt. This eccentric chase continued until the possum spun around in a rage.

"STOP FUCKING FOLLOWING ME!"

"You use that word a lot, you know. You should consider expanding your vocabulary." One might imagine the hare placing one front paw over another and cocking its head to the side with haughtiness were it still possible. It is to be lamented the best it could do was raise one eyebrow and look down its nose in a superior fashion.

"I'll give you one thing," said the possum. "You gotta lot of nerve. What makes you so damn proud? You're nothing but a head!"

"And you, I might point out, are nothing but a loosely organized collection of bones. I'm not sure I would trade my position for yours, even if such were possible. But getting back to my original question. What will you do if the bear does not cease its roaring, which I will be the first to admit is both unnerving and uncouth. You hardly appear to be in any fit state to challenge it, but perhaps you think you could do a better job of being king."

"King? Ain't got no interest in any such thing. And who said anything about anyone being a king to begin with?"

"Chancellor or president, alpha or prime minister, or any other term of high office you prefer then. The bear has been appointed our leader and one should always respect one's betters."

"Appointed? Says who? Standing up and making pretty speeches and shouting out orders don't make you king."

"And I suppose you think you would be a better candidate. What exactly have you done for the cause?"

"I'm getting around to it. Can't rush these things."

"Ah, here is a point of agreement between us. It doesn't do to *hare* about in such a hurly-burly fashion, does it?" The hare tittered at its own little jest. "One must maintain some decorum even amidst revolutionary times such as these."

"Yeah, you're doing a great job." The possum snickered.

"I am doing my best," replied the hare with the sort of plaintive dignity that can only be expressed by a severed head hanging from a heron's beak by one bedraggled ear. "I fear our acquaintanceship has gotten off to a poor beginning. Maybe if we introduced ourselves. I am Lysander. I've not had a chance to get this noble bird's moniker—"

"BRRT," burped the bird, dropping the hare head.

"Dear me. Excuse you, I'm sure," Lysander said in a muffled voice, having most unfortunately rolled to a stop face down. "Do you have indigestion?"

"Nope. Name. Burt," explained the heron succinctly, adding "sorry" as it bent and scooped up the hare by its other ear.

"Ah, I see," said Lysander, shaking its head in a bobbling attempt at regaining its equilibrium. "Burt? Really? I would have expected something more poetic for such a magnificent figure of a bird, but never mind. And you, sir? Or madam perchance?"

"I dunno," said the possum. "Ma called me Po, but she called all thirteen of us Po."

"Do you mean to say she produced thirteen offspring? Most prodigious."

"Naw. Pretty regular stuff."

"I call it noble. Well, it seems, Po, we are expected to contribute something to the mighty undertaking unfolding around us. What do you think we should do?"

"I dunno. I guess I could do some biting and clawing. What about you?"

"Biting, yes, if, er, Burt can get me close enough. Sadly, I have misplaced my claws."

"Yeah, I can see that. Where's the rest of you?"

"Last I saw, it was lying in the wildwoods border back there a ways." Lysander rolled its eyes to indicate a possible direction for investigation.

"Lessee." Po skittered off, followed closely by bird and hare.

It took some doing, with Po parting the long grasses with claws and toothy grin, and Lysander somewhat fretfully and impatiently directing the heron to swing it this way and that, but the hare's body was at last located.

"Fucking hell. Look at the state of you," said the possum. "Too bad you can't attach it back. Be a helluva lot more convenient than hanging around."

"A most intriguing notion," Lysander replied. "If only we knew a weaver bird or even a shrike. They are excellent tailors. They might be able to use pine needles or reeds."

"Like these?" The possum tore loose some thin reeds which were growing from the murky water collected in a nearby ditch. They bent easily in its boney hands without breaking. It poked one experimentally through the neck of the body of the hare. "Might could see what I can do." Po tore Lysander's head from the heron's beak.

"I say, I say, I say..." the hare stuttered. "I say, I say."

"Don't lose your head. Oh, right, too late for that, ain't it?" Po cackled, weaving the reeds in and out. "Don't hurt, do it?"

"No, I am gratified to report it isn't painful, but it is most undignified and unlikely to produce the desired result, wouldn't you say?"

"Can't be more undignified than what you got now. Worth a try, don't you think, Burt?"

"Yup," said the heron, clacking its beak enthusiastically—after all, it is rather tiresome to be without use of one's mouth and tongue because you are carrying around a hare's head by one ear.

The possum's clever though boney paws made short work of the repair job, tying off the last reed with a complicated knot.

"How's it feel?"

"My my," Lysander said, rolling its eyes about to try and see the rest of its body. "I do believe I can move, even hop a little."

The hare suited action to words, making ungainly short jumps while its head bobbled alarmingly but held fast. "How unexpected, but a much more convenient method of locomotion, although I appreciate your efforts very much, of course, er, Burt."

"Sure. Go stab now," the heron replied, making alarming darting dagger motions with its long, sharp beak and stalking away toward the sounds of mayhem, which were never far away.

"I don't like to complain," said Lysander into the awkward moment which followed the heron's departure, "but I think you might have been a bit more careful when reattaching my head. I do believe you've put it on backwards."

"I ain't no fucking expert at reattaching heads, am I?"

"Quite. That is self-evident." The hare attempted to move forward but, in its confusion, found itself moving backward. "Possibly you could try again?"

Po picked at the reeds a moment. "Did a good job with this knot. Don't think I can unpick it. Could gnaw through maybe, given enough time."

"How bothersome, but I suppose I'll have to make do. We should join in with the others or we'll be too late."

"You think? There's a fuckton of humans."

"Far more of us though, wouldn't you think?"

"Yeah, I guess. So, maybe we ain't really needed if there's only so many humans to go around. Let the others have their fun."

Lysander crossed its paws and looked as thoughtful as a hare with a backwards head could reasonably look. "There is something in what you say. I've had a trying time of it, what with one thing and another. I think I will sit here and rest awhile. You may keep me company, if you like."

The possum stretched, skeleton clacking and creaking. "My bones could use a breather, I guess," it said, settling down beside the hare.

Time passed. Lightning flashed. Unearthly noises were heard. The hare hummed a tune both uncanny yet soothing to the ear.

Po thought it might have brought tears to the eyes if it still had them. The possum cleared what was once its throat. "You're an okay guy. I feel kind of bad. I knew I was putting your head on wrong. Meant it as a joke."

The hare nodded, head drooping and wobbling alarmingly. "I thought as much. I didn't think it was possible you wouldn't notice, but I forgive you."

"Ah, fuck, come here."

Long into the night, the subtle sound of sharp teeth chewing through tough reeds was heard.

Human: Lise

Jenny and I escape out the back door of the church. I wanted to stay. Wanted it to be over, but she pinched and prodded and pulled with such desperation that I found myself stumbling after her. It's surprisingly quiet and peaceful in the parking lot. I guess the animals are busy inside for the time being. I try not to think about what must be happening in there.

"We have to get out of town," Jenny whispers vehemently.

"What's the point? They'll find us wherever we go."

"They're attacking places where people gather. What if we go off into the woods? My uncle's cabin is way out by Blender's Bluff. Not another soul around for miles and miles."

I scoff. "Like the woods aren't full of animals."

"Not dead ones. Not killed by humans. Didn't you notice every animal we've seen is injured? Tire marks, guts out. Roadkill."

Roadkill. Such a descriptive word except they weren't killed by the road, but by the humans who built it and used it with such carelessness for any other form of life. I even knew families who ate what they hit. Hey, we're country folk through and through. It happens. Could make an argument that it's better than letting the meat go to waste in these hard times.

"There's probably animals killed by humans in the woods too," I remind her.

"Not as many. Most hunters around here eat their kills. With food so scarce, they don't leave them lying around waiting to come back as zombies. It's worth a try anyway. Would you rather stay here and get torn apart?"

Yes, I want desperately to say.

I used to speculate idly on what I would do when the apocalypse came (I said I was a pessimist). I'd decided long ago I'd want to be mowed down in the first wave of whatever it was instead of being one of those ragtag, grimly determined survivors we're supposed to cheer on in movies and tv shows. I'd always thought they were losers. Most of them died anyway in the end. Why prolong the agony?

But there's Jenny, looking at me with those big brown eyes of hers and a firmness to her jaw she gets when she's passionately set on something. Most stubborn girl I ever knew, but something in me doesn't want her to be alone at the end. The least I can do is try and keep her company. So, if she's determined to go, I'll go with her for as long and as far as we can get. I owe her that much.

Partially-Digested Squirrel

It's so dark. Don't remember how I got here but it's awful. Dark and smelly and... and... *gooshy*.

Gotta pull myself together. Literally. Why am I in so many pieces? What happened to me?

Me. Who is me? Don't remember that either. Shit. This isn't good.

Ok ok ok... stay calm. There's some kind of opening there. Let's try crawling a little at a time. Anything has to be better than sloshing around in this gunk.

Seem to have triggered something. The walls are convulsing around me... us... whatever...

Fuck, I think it's gonna blow. Here we goooooooooooooooooooooooooooooo...

...

...

...

Wow. That was a wild ride. At least now there's some light. Smooth white walls but no ceiling. Dammit, there are pieces of me everywhere swimming in this nasty water. What the hell happened to me?

What's that up above? It's a human. A fucking human. I should've known. Any time shit goes down, it's always humans. If I was in better shape, I'd give that dumb motherfucker what for.

Wait, what's it reaching for? No, don't. I like it here ok. I take back what I said. Don't do that. What's that noise? Where's the water going?

Oh, crap...

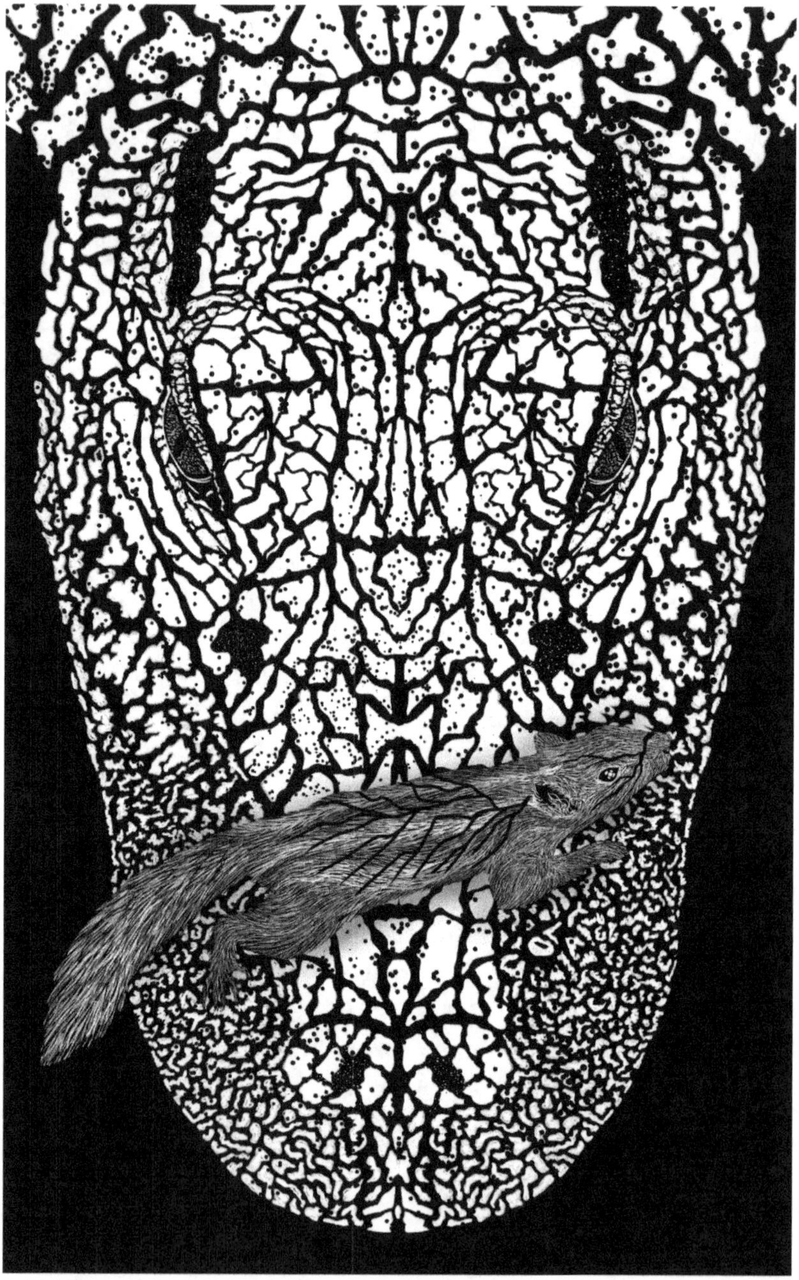

Gator (and Chipmunk)

The gator is all sluggish thought, reptilian-brained, slow to react but deadly when roused to action. The chipmunk is a giggler, a prankster. Brain the size of a pea but not a cell of it wasted.

Clever, thinks the gator, watching the flattened thing dance about.

It pelts humans with nuts and acorns. Does them little harm but adds to their fear and confusion. Gator enjoys watching. But the chipmunk pesters her: *Join in, join in! Let 'em have it!*

She's clumsy without the long tail which anchored her, balanced her, added weight and thrust to her explosive attacks, but humans are easy prey. Most stand frozen as she approaches, mouths hanging open, making feeble movements with their stick-like arms.

Foolish, she dubs them. She never once had fear of them in life, and in death, is only angry with a burning fury at the mockery they have made of her once perfect form. She may not have her lovely, lovely tail, but she has teeth and jaws to clamp on with a fearful force and never let go.

Look at you! Look at you! Look at you go! the chipmunk chatters, squealing with delight at the sight of the humans twisting and flopping and begging for mercy where they have shown none.

The gator is all sluggish thought, but one screams louder than the others: *kill*

Trout

The trout could not help but think it was having a not very good day. First, something vile had floated downstream from the human place with all the smoke. It made the water greasy and foul, choking out breath. Just as it had swum upstream past the nastiness, it had been chased by an otter, sleek and wily, only to be plucked to a kind of safety by a loud, ill-smelling bird. Being unused to flying, the fish had struggled against claws and queasiness as it surveyed the fields passing below with nausea-inducing speed.

As if that weren't enough, something startled the bird. A long and terrifying fall ensued, punctuated by the bumper of a red '75 Chevy pickup which had been restored to pristine condition, a fact which was lost upon the trout as it lay flopping out its death throes among the prickly burrs along the side of the road.

Now night had fallen and there was some kind of uproar around that it couldn't quite see except in rapid movements just out of view from time to time. Unpleasant noises. Stench. The absence of the cool splendid wetness of its natural home. And the feeling it ought to be doing *something*. That *something* was expected of it, but it had no way to comply even if it could decide what that *something* was.

Yes, taking everything into consideration, this was a very bad day and it showed no signs of ending. Nothing to do but lay and flop and think fishy thoughts and wait to see what happened next.

Human: Lise

Somehow, we make it through town by keeping watch from the backstreets and looking for opportunities to slip through the chaos. It's Jenny who notices the animals (for lack of a better description—that or *things*, so many of them are unrecognizable as anything but monsters) are sweeping in a semi-organized fashion from the northside of town to the south. Suits us. The cabin's to the north, so if we can get behind enemy lines, so to speak, we might have a chance.

Nearly lost it when we almost ran right into a grey wolf who blended in with the night. Luckily, it's distracted by what I think is a fox, though its fur, once as red as Jenny's hair, is so bedraggled and dirty, it's hard to tell for sure. If I didn't know better, I might think the fox and wolf were arguing, though I don't know why that would be stranger than anything else we'd seen. Once you've accepted one impossible thing, might as well swallow everything else whole.

"Lise!" Jenny hisses at me more than once as I linger behind, lost in my own world, overwhelmed. It's her who urges me on again and again. I wouldn't keep going for anyone else. Maybe it's my lingering guilt over my rejection of her. Our small town doesn't take kindly to anyone different, anything they consider *unnatural*. No matter how often we discussed and argued, I wasn't brave enough to be out and open in a relationship that would make us targets.

But I do love her, love beyond reason, love which should have been enough when life was normal, but it's that love which keeps me with her now death feels near. Those people I'd been so afraid of are lying in pieces around us as we creep along our escape route, and what I feel isn't mourning or loss but a sense of freedom I've never had before. It's me and Jenny against the world, just as she'd always wanted. Her hand warm and firm in mine. It'd be an exaggeration to say I'd never been so happy in my life, but I had never felt more at ease with our togetherness.

And all it took was the end of the world.

Feral Piglets

follow mama follow mama
itch scratch JUMP
bump their rumps
and watch them run
was there ever so much fun?

follow mama follow mama
do as mama does
scrape and bite
rip and tear
toss the pieces here and there

follow mama follow mama
chase them near and far
make them trip
make them wallow
listen to them hoot and holler

follow mama follow mama
she's calling to us now
stay together little ones
endless work yet to be done
was there ever so much fun?

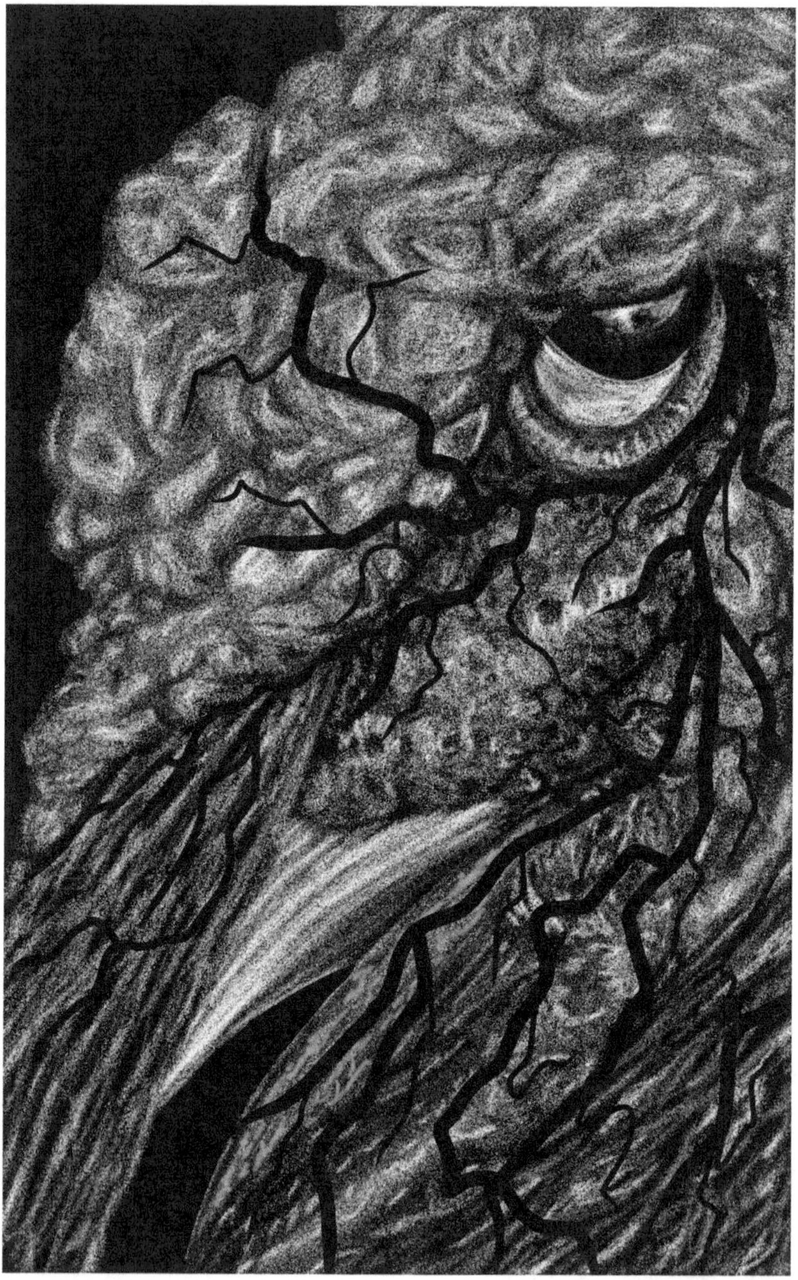

Turkey and Trout

What's up?

You are. Would you mind not towering over me like that? It's a little intimidating and I've already had a terrible day. The worst.

You're a fish.

Yes?

A fish out of water.

Yes. What are you?

Tom turkey, of course. Haven't you ever seen one?

No. As you pointed out, I'm a fish which means I spend my life underwater. Do turkeys live underwater?

That's a laugh! A turkey living underwater like a fish. Can you imagine me bobbing around like a fat old pumpkin. That's a good one!

Hey! Would you mind not hitting me?

Just giving you a friendly pat. Slap on the back. For your joke. Best I heard all night.

I wouldn't think many would be joking on a night like this.

You'd be surprised. Some folks got a weird sense of humor. But what else are we gonna do in such a situation? I mean, look at the state of my poor head.

I had noticed, of course, but didn't think it was polite to mention it.

Couldn't help but notice, could you? Course I can't see it but it don't feel right.

It's... it's not quite as bad as it could be.

Yeah? Good to hear. Appreciate it, pal. Say, you're not in such good shape yourself. Anything I can do for you?

I don't suppose...

Yes?

Could you manage to carry me back to water of some kind? I know it doesn't really matter anymore, but it feels terrible being out here exposed. I'd like to feel at home again before whatever is going to happen happens.

Why? What's gonna happen?

I don't know, but something, don't you think? I don't see how we can go on this way forever. Can't you feel the power in this storm? Do you think it might have something to do with us? And no storm lasts forever. What'll happen when it's over?

Hey, you might be onto something there. You're pretty smart for a fish. I always thought fish were dumb, but you got brains.

I was at the top of my school.

School?

A fish joke.

Oh, I get it! Good one! You're a regular comedian. Way to keep your spirits up! I saw a nice little pool not too far from here. Got some pretty fish in it. Fancy things. Frilly. Would that suit?

It would be so kind of you.

No problem. You've given me a good laugh and something to think on. What happens next, eh? What happens next...

Wolf

The bear is a fool. He fails to grasp the larger opportunity this conflict presents. I strike down humans naturally, as we are called to do on this night, but I do not neglect to kill any other living creature who crosses my path, from the chained-up dog cowering in its little house to a herd of deer frozen in fear at my might. I may only be half the creature I once was, but what teeth and claws I have left retain their expertise.

In this way, our company of the dead grows and grows. For we must outnumber not only the humans but the living animals, else they will turn upon us as soon as the human threat is eliminated. I see how they look at us, flee in fear. We are as much an enemy in their eyes as the humans ever were.

Not all, but enough of the others are sympathetic to my point of view and assist my plans. Our newly-turned soldiers are loyal to their makers. When the time is right, it is I who will rule and the bear who will take orders from me or be destroyed utterly, for I am as patient and sure as the sun rising in the morning.

Human: Lise

We're almost out of town when we hear the crying. A little boy. Pale skin and blond buzzcut, dirty and cut up with shallow scratches and dried blood. Neither Jenny or me recognize him, but he can't be more than three or four. I've never been good at guessing kids' ages, but he looks too young to understand what's happening (not that we do either). Old enough to be scared out of his wits though.

I'm bigger and stronger than Jenny so I grab him up in my arms, hardly stopping. The woods are in sight, and we aren't gonna let ourselves get distracted, but we can't leave him alone either. I'm afraid he won't shut up and will attract attention to us, but he must be exhausted, 'cause he hiccups a few times against my neck and then goes quiet. Not asleep but content now an adult is in the picture. Most kids can't imagine there's any problem an adult can't fix, right? I wish.

The last bit's the worst. We have to come right out in the open and cross the highway to get to the woods. We wait a long time hidden in some bushes, looking up and down the road as far as we can see. The lightning above is nearly constant, but it's like sheet lightning. Lights up the sky rather than striking anywhere I can tell, but it makes creepy shadows. Impossible to tell for sure if there's anything, alive or dead, moving around us.

Finally, Jenny gives a signal and we break out in a slow jog, tempted to rush but not wanting to be loud enough on the pavement to attract unwelcome notice. We reach the shelter of the pines and brush on the other side safe enough, though Jenny swears she saw a big turkey with some kind of fish draped across its back strutting down the middle of the road as we crossed. At this point, I'd believe anything, so I don't even question it.

The woods sound alive, but they always do. A thousand creatures on the move, but I'm counting on the fact it's only the dead ones we need to fear. I hope Jenny was right that their attack is focused on town. It's the only thing that might give us a chance. We face a good three- or four-hour hike to her uncle's cabin. Maybe more—it's hard to say. We usually drive up there, but we'd already agreed the noise of starting up an engine was dangerous. We'd seen too many wrecked cars on the road. They seem to be magnets for the wrath of the animals.

Taking one last look back at everything we're leaving behind, I settle the boy more comfortably on my hip and follow Jenny into the wilderness.

Roadkill

I watch them go. Two girls. One's carrying something but I'm too far away to see what. Thought about chasing after them, but what's the fucking point?

I'm different from these animals. They won't accept me. Would kill me if I weren't already dead. Guess dying's the only halfway smart thing I ever done.

Point is, I got the urge to kill same as these other sorry creatures, but I can't win 'em over that way. I was human once. That's enough for them to shun me, even if I met the same shitty end they did.

Before I died, I was living rough a year or two (hard to keep track when you don't have a calendar or phone or even a watch). Long as I stayed in the deep woods, it was safe enough. But you gotta get supplies sometimes. I usually raided houses out from town. Took a little of this, little of that. Enough to keep me going but not enough to be missed. Didn't want to attract cops. They'd beat me up and see me down the road to the next town if I was lucky. Worse, if not.

Always went raiding at night but wasn't careful enough. Course they was driving without lights. Drunk off their asses maybe. Swerved right toward me then kept on going. Never stopped, never checked. Probably thought they hit a deer.

So that's me. Roadkill, but not wanted on either side of this war. Turns out death ain't much different than life. Not for me. I stand in the road and look toward town, then toward the woods where those girls disappeared. Two directions and not welcome in either. Which way would you go?

Dog and Cat

Scene: large and powerful yellow DOG of indeterminate breed with caked blood upon its head trots with purpose as a fat orange tabby CAT crawling with maggots ambles along behind, stopping often to investigate random scents, before running wildly to catch up to the dog again.

DOG thoughts: I pride myself on my road savvy. My masters always let me run free. Free to roam all over town and menace dogs smaller and milder than myself. I tower over most. 180 pounds of pure muscle. Even the humans scattered when they saw me coming. Lord of the streets was I—until a moment of distraction. Stupid cat. Hasn't a sensible thought in its brain, assuming it has one. Darting out in front of a car like that. Instinct made me snatch it back but too late for us both.

CAT thoughts: Dog good. Follow dog. Oooh, what's this?

DOG thoughts: Look at the pathetic thing. Won't leave me alone, but I've no time to worry about it. We've been given permission to do what I've been bred for. To hunt, to bite, to devour. How foolish the masters are, my own and these others. They scramble for guns, empty kitchen drawers of knives, arm themselves with baseball bats, those silly sticks they use for a very silly game. Almost as bad as fetch. Fetch, I ask you. I always refused to go along with that one. I am no man's servant.

CAT thoughts: Poop. It was poop. Nice.

DOG thoughts: There's another one. Shooting at us won't do any good. (BARKS) Ha, look at him run. I'll give him a head start. Makes the kill even sweeter. What... what is that cat doing?

CAT thoughts: Dog butt smells nice.

DOG sighs.

An interlude. DOG scratches one ear with hind leg. CAT licks a paw and rubs it over face, knocking off stray maggots. Picks one up and tastes it. Makes a face.

DOG speaks: You're disgusting.

CAT speaks: Thank you, Dog.

DOG thoughts: What a loon. Think it's about time to play my own game of fetch.

DOG breaks into a dead run. Flushes man from behind a car that has crashed into a tree by the side of the road. Tears out the man's throat. DOG howls in triumph over the corpse. CAT inspects it, claws an eyeball from out of its socket.

CAT speaks: Neat. Good dog.

DOG speaks: Stupid cat.

Fox

The fox pads along, solitary. Enough fur and meat remain to cushion her skeleton from the sharp gravel on the road beneath her paws, if she could feel it. Her once proud red fur hangs in tatters here and there, enough for her to be recognizable for the sleek and sly beauty who once haunted the few remnants of the ancient woods left to nature by humans.

She is a secret, silent thing, slipping here and there, leading by example rather than speeches or sly words. Her teeth are as sharp as they were in life and as efficient. She's noticed her fellow dead have unnatural strength. They need it in their bruised and battered forms. She idly marks each one as she passes them. Makes note of their species and injuries and whether there is enough of their bodies left to be of practical use to the mission. Appreciates those who can only cheer and encourage. They serve too in their way.

She has no illusions. The bear sees it as a majestic cause he was destined to lead. Makes every victory about himself. Wants to be remembered and revered as a hero.

And the grey wolf? He is a villain through and through. She knows this of old.

What she makes of the night's eldritch work and the future, she keeps to herself, but she has many thoughts, many thoughts...

Human: Lise

The hike feels endless. A rugged fight through brush with only the near constant electricity from the storm to light the way. We hadn't had time to gather any supplies, so the only lucky thing to happen all night is when we stumble across a homeless camp. No one's around, so we grab some bottled water and pack a few cans of food into a used plastic grocery bag. We still have a long way to go, so we leave more than we take. Too heavy to carry. Besides, it doesn't feel good stealing from someone with so little, if they aren't dead already.

We've been walking for hours when the sky starts to lighten up. It's a relief to be able to see better and to think the sun might be going to come up on another day after all. The weird lightning is still going, but it doesn't seem as angry somehow, like it's running out of steam. We spot animals from time to time, but living ones who are as scared of us as we are wary of them. They scatter and scurry away, which is more the natural order of things and gives us hope.

The boy wakes up when I have to set him down to get some relief in my back. His wide blue eyes look up at us as we try to talk to him. He's either too young or too scared to speak.

"What's your name?" I ask, tired of referring to him or thinking of him as "the boy," but he just stares at me.

"Tell you what," says Jenny. "We'll give you a special name just for us to use. How about that? What do you think it should be, Lise?"

One springs to mind right away. A name I'd toyed with for myself when I'd thought about moving away from our nowhere town to some place they never heard of me. Where introducing myself as Cyrus might raise fewer eyebrows, though I'd have to change my appearance too, I guess. Isn't what's inside for most people. They only care what you look like on the outside. But no, Cyrus was special. Even here at the end of the world, I'd save the name for a future me who would never be.

"What about Enoch?" I suggest instead.

"Enoch?" Jenny laughs, such a pure, clear sound after the horrors we've witnessed and heard, I can't help grinning back at her. "Couldn't you think of anything that isn't better suited to a couple of centuries ago?"

"What's wrong with Enoch? Got a vibe to it. We can shorten it to E. Cool, right?"

The boy smiles at me. "E!" he shouts, startling a nearby bird into noisy flight.

"Shush!" Jenny scolds, looking around nervously.

His smile fades.

"It's ok, honey," I say. "We're playing a game. Be as quiet as we can, right? Right, E?"

He nods his head solemnly and whispers "E" so softly, I can hardly hear it.

I grin again, picking him up and giving him a hug so he can't see the tears in my eyes. I'm sadder for him than me or Jenny. At least we'd lived long enough to experience a few things. I'm scared as hell E won't get the same chance.

What a messed-up world it was even before this latest madness. Like everything was spiraling out of control or grinding to a halt, one or the other or both at once. Life getting harder and harder for everyone but the richest year after year. It couldn't go on that way forever, but you still never expect it to end. Not really. Not like this.

Flora and Stanley

"Come and Witness the Dynamic Duo!" read the flyers at Simpson's Animal Rescue. Flora, an emu, and Stanley, a capuchin monkey, were inseparable and quite the celebrities, locally and beyond. Videos of the emu stalking around the farm while the adorable monkey clung to her back and neck were big hits online. Brought the sanctuary in most of their donations if the truth be told, so it was a catastrophe when Flora and Stanley escaped their enclosure and went on a ten-hour adventure which ended only when they were struck and killed by an eighteen-wheeler. Their bodies were never recovered, flung deep into the woods to molder. Inseparable in life and in death.

They were both extremely puzzled to be brought back to a kind of living so many weeks later, shadows of their former selves, but content to still be together in whatever this new thing was. Being a member of a clan of stubborn and ornery birds, the emu had no intention of joining in whatever was happening in the town, but no way were they going back to the sanctuary either. The things that had gone on there behind closed doors when the cameras were turned off didn't bear remembering.

Stanley hoped the vast graveyard hidden in a remote field out of view of visitors was full of vengeful beings. Could they unearth themselves? The burial plots were shallow after all. He wouldn't have minded going and checking it out, joining in the mayhem, but where Flora went, Stanley went, so he'd never know for sure if their old tormentors had gotten their richly-deserved rewards.

Where Flora went was deeper into the woods, her big, ungainly body stalking through brush and low-hanging branches as if they were scenery cut from cardboard and tissue paper for a most unusual theater production. Stanley bent low, hugging what remained of Flora in a fierce grip so as to avoid being flung off. She was no longer the warm and softly plush ride of old, but then he was no longer terribly cute, so allowances must be made on both sides.

It was dark and peaceful in the forest. The monkey looked up, catching sight of the green sky and faint lightning flashes far above. After a time, here and there a break in the clouds let a star or two peep in and the dark took on a different quality, like those moments before sunrise where the faintest hints of color hold promise of a new day. He wondered what it would bring, but as long as he was with Flora, nothing else mattered.

Geese

gabble honk hiss honk
some think we're nothing
but a mean gaggle of bastards
ain't gonna take shit from no one
animal or human
we'll tell you that much for nothing
gibble gabble hiss and honk motherfuckers

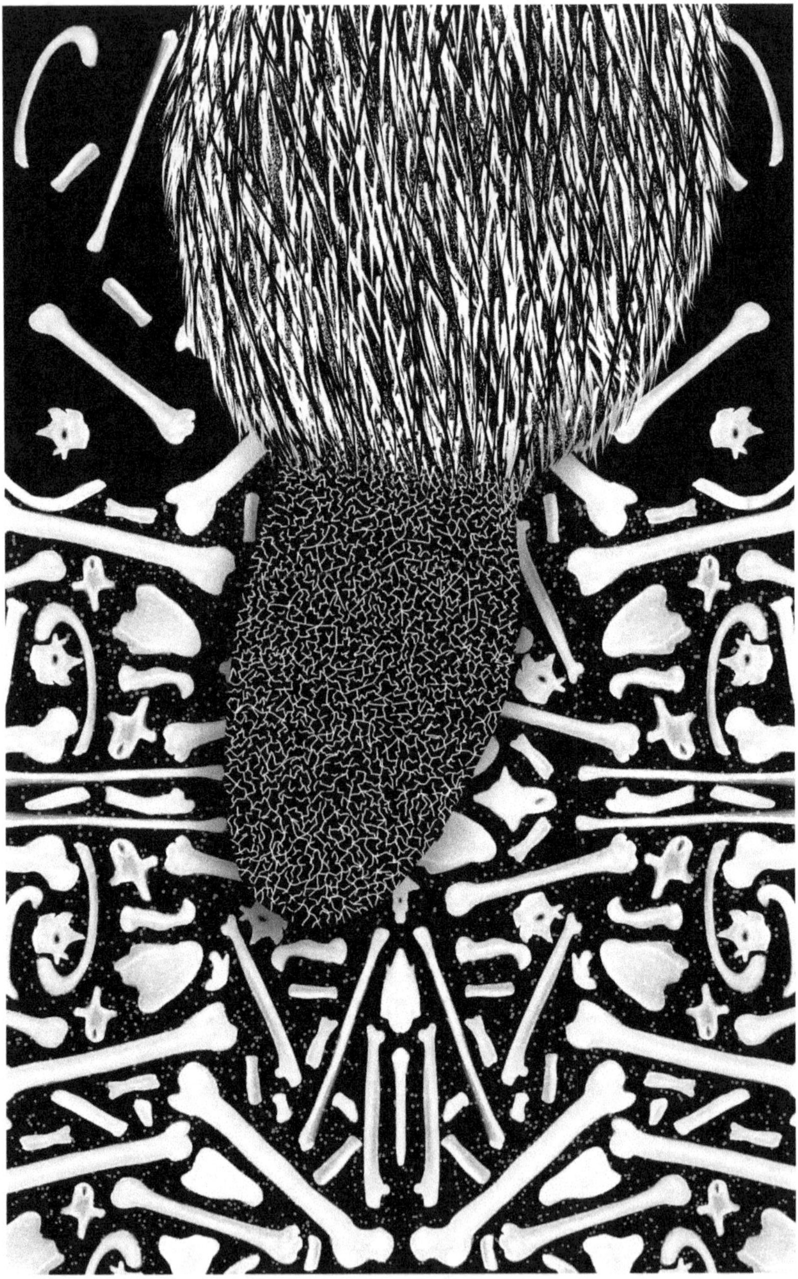

Mr. and Mrs. Beaver

"Look here, Mother. Some more for our collection."

"Aren't you a clever clogs, Father. Such lovely white sticks as you're collecting this night. Our den this winter will be the strongest we've ever had."

"Ah, it will be a night to remember, won't it, luv?"

"Such goings on as we've never seen. One could almost feel sorry for the poor things."

"They do make a dreadful noise when I collect their sticks."

"Dreadful. I can hear it from here. How goes the campaign?"

"Must be pretty good—listen. Fewer screams."

"You're right. Must be nearing the end I should think, but that's alright. I think we've had our share, haven't we, Father?"

"Yes, don't want to be greedy, do we?"

"No, my dear. Especially as we've no little ones to think of nor ever likely to again in our condition, but no use dwelling on things as can't be mended. You know what would be useful? A few more of these smaller sticks. They're good for filling in the gaps."

"Right you are! Plenty of those to be had. I'll go see what I can find, shall I?"

"You are a right one, Father, and no mistake. C'mere and give us a kiss before you go."

"Here you are, luv. One for the road and one as a promise for later."

"Go on with you!"

Human: Jenny

I can't believe it.

We were close, so close. It's my fault. I'd gotten careless, excited to be almost to the cabin, finally seeing familiar landmarks. I rushed ahead, too far ahead, so when I hear Lise's cry, I'm not near enough to help her.

I retrace my steps, running harder than I ever have in my life, but it's too late. She's on the ground, being stomped on by this huge bird-like thing. Some smaller creature has its arms wrapped around E's neck, choking him. I grab up a fallen branch, and swing it as hard as I can, knocking the bird's head way off into the woods. The rest of its body seems to give up without the head, slamming down on top of Lise.

The thing around the boy's neck screeches and leaps at me. Grasping, boney fingers reach for my face. I bat it away with the branch and when it scrambles back toward me, catch it by the skull and rip it from the body, throwing it as far as I can. Like the bird, the body collapses without the head and dissolves into a pathetic little heap of bone and muscle. I've always had a soft spot for animals and can't help feeling a twinge of compassion and guilt. I have to remind myself these things are no longer animals but monsters.

Rushing over to Lise, I use the branch as leverage and manage to roll the bird's body off her with a lot of effort 'cause it weighs a ton. Long, bloody gashes rake across Lise's stomach, and I catch glimpses of stuff spilling out that I'd rather not see where the wounds are deepest.

"FUCK!" she spits out and I must be hysterical because I can't help an involuntary snort of laughter through my tears. I can count on one hand the number of times I've ever heard Lise swear. "Is it bad?" she asks.

"It's not good, but you're still alive."

"Um, yeah..." she winces. "Listen, there may be more of those things. Take E and get to the cabin. You'll have more of a chance there than out here in the open."

"No, I'm not leaving you like this. We need bandages and antiseptics. There's a first aid kit in the cabin."

"Jenny, listen to me! I don't think a first aid kit is gonna do a whole lot in this situation. If it was just the two of us, it wouldn't matter so much. But E deserves a chance. He's only a kid."

I glance over at the boy who's staring at Lise in wide-eyed wonder. I'm guessing it's not the first awful thing he's seen tonight, or maybe he's in shock and not really taking it in. I'm ready to fight Lise. After all, E is some kid we happened to pick up. We don't know anything about him. Not even his real name. Whereas Lise... Lise knows what she is to me.

Before I can argue though, she closes her eyes, letting out a soft little puff of breath I'd never of heard if I hadn't been bent so close to her.

"Lise, Lise," I call just as softly. This moment feels sacred, like the fate of the world depends on whether she answers me or not. Like the whole course of the rest of my life is about to be decided and I have absolutely no say in it, no control.

I hear E whimpering softly. The leaves rustle above in the trees and below where they've fallen along the forest floor. The repetitive call of some insect—Lise would be able to tell me what kind it was. She always knew stuff like that. Small frogs chirping. A keening birdsong.

All these things I hear before I hear one more sound from my beloved.

Bear

By and large, my soldiers are performing magnificently. A few stragglers and malingerers as is only to be expected during such an immense undertaking. It matters little as we outnumber our enemy greatly, so I can readily forgive those who are in no shape or have no inclination to engage. Most cheer us on all the same. It is a pleasure to see how united we are in this effort when one considers that many of the members of my army were natural enemies, one to another, in life.

The red fox has not revealed her name, but the grey wolf is Asha. Both have proven able lieutenants, running here and there as best they can, bearing in mind their considerable injuries, and reporting back to me on skirmishes beyond my view.

There is something about the wolf I cannot like. He has a lean and hungry look, what is left of him, and speaks to me with something not far short of contempt at times. I must keep an eye on him. This is neither the time nor place for conspiracies or disrespect. Discipline must be maintained if we are to accomplish our objectives before sunrise, for I have a feeling the return of the sun will bring about a change. Of what kind, I cannot say, but every shattered bone in my body whispers the same warning: we must hurry.

Snake

It is long and black and sleek. A pretty thing, if lamentably flat here and there. It once dwelled in the human's basement, keeping the mice and rats at bay—a most useful service. Never once witnessed the sun set or rise with its own two eyes, but you don't miss what you know nothing of. A nice little life in the dark until the men came.

Confusion. Shouts. Hands reaching. *Catch it, boys. Catch it and kill it. There it goes...*

Escape. Relief but short-lived. Not familiar with roads and cars. Doesn't know to be careful. Ah, well...

It has a second chance at a kind of life now. Part of it thinks to remain harmless to any but its traditional prey, but there is an urge rising and rising from the tip of its tail, along the glittering scales which line its ruined body and into the dim, instinctual recesses of its brain. *Let us hunt and kill a different kind of prey...*

It slinks along with the crowd. Has never seen so many nor so many different types of creatures. Does not know the names for more than a few, but senses they have common purpose, confirmed when what it learns later is called a bear grabs it by the tail and flings it at a human.

To fly through the air like a winged thing! The snake would laugh if it knew how. Exhilarating.

The bear has good aim. The snake lands on a man's shoulder. The man screams and grabs, but the snake is swift and sure. This human is a thousand times the size of a mouse, but the theory is the same. Wrap and wrap around the neck, cut off breath. All things must breathe (*unless you are already a dead thing*). It only takes time and patience.

The human pries and pokes with meaty, beefy fingers. Eyes bulge, face reddens. It can't believe it, can it? Such a fuss.

What a waste holed up those years in one place. The snake never even had a chance to find a mate, one like itself. Eggs. Children. Progenitor of a new generation and generations to come. Missed opportunities.

The snake cranes its neck from side to side as it waits for the end of the man it holds in its coils. Watches the sky from a better vantage point than it has ever enjoyed and wonders if it will have a chance to witness its first dawn. The larger world has turned out to be much more interesting than it could ever have imagined. If these startlingly novel experiences are what it can expect in its new incarnation, it thinks it a good enough trade.

Mourning Doves

My mate is a wondrous thing. Grey-feathered, soft as soft, and as plump as ever he was. He spreads a shattered wing over my back to shield me from the blood which flies from these horrid battles we witness. We are as timid as we were in life. Not timid, he says, but cautious and careful. We are not fighters but lovers. We feel the anger that rises, same as the others, but it is a distant thing for us, secondary to the only thing that has ever mattered. We two. Breast to breast, necks entwined. Cooing our soft ballads to one another. So we lived together and so we died together and together we are still. I am blessed.

My mate is a marvel. Her depthless dark eyes take in the dreadful scenes around us yet lose none of their sweet innocence. Would that I could spare her such sights. I failed to keep her safe. Led her directly into the path of danger, but she says she would not want it any other way. Our fates are tied together. Have been since the day we met on the high branches of the old oak tree where we made our first nest. Raised many a clutch before our end. I hope our children fly free and have found their own soul mates. For what greater happiness can there be than to know another inside and out and for them to know you? This is all. The rest is noise, distraction. Oh, my darling, we are joined for eternity. I am blessed.

Human: Jenny

"Jenny?"

I gasp. Stare into those hazel eyes I know so well. Push the unruly black curls back from her forehead. "Lise?"

"Cyrus."

"What? Who's Cyrus?"

"I am. At least, I always wanted to be. I think I've been reborn, so shouldn't I get to be Cyrus this time around if I want?"

"What are you talking about? Reborn?"

She sits up abruptly, unnaturally bending from the waist without even using the strength of her arms to help her. She stands just as abruptly, all one movement. So swift, I can hardly take it in. A single strand of something that shouldn't drops from the rips in her clothing. Dangles there obscenely until she hastily tucks it back into her flannel shirt, tying the tails in a tight knot to keep it there.

"You know what I'm talking about," she says. "I'm like the others now."

There's a kind of pity in her eyes as she watches my face, sees the moment when I get it. I thought it a miracle she was still alive, but she isn't. She's one of the dead. But that's its own kind of miracle, isn't it? I still have my Lise… or…

"Cyrus?" E asks. "That your name? You okay?"

It's the most he's said and proves at least he can talk.

"She's fine," I try to assure him, not sure how much he understands about what's going on.

"He."

I turn to Lise. "What?"

"Could you use he instead of she? And Cyrus instead of Lise? Do you mind?"

"No, of course not, but… you never said anything before."

"I was afraid to. Like I was afraid of everything. Of us. Of what people would think. Of being different. Of losing you, even just as a friend."

"You'll never lose me. I love you, whoever you are."

"Even like this?" He gestures down at his torn shirt.

"Even now. Always." I grab him in a hug, tentatively at first, but he's still warm to the touch, the same as in life, and doesn't seem to be in any pain. I sob and cling to him as though I'll die too if I ever let go.

Human: Cyrus

The worst has come. Well, not the worst, I guess. It would be much worse if Jenny had died instead of me. If it had to be one of us, I'm glad it worked out this way. And the way she accepted my true name! She slipped up once, but a change like that after you've known someone your whole life takes some getting used to. Her pink cheeks flushed red and she stuttered an apology, but it's more important to me that the look she gives me, the one I'm so used to, the look which says "you are the one for me," hasn't dimmed one bit.

What a lot of time I wasted when I was alive. That's me. Always doing things backwards or too late. Hard to remember being so afraid all the time now. Nothing like being dead to give you courage. And I still feel the same about her, but it's like the memory of a dream which is already starting to fade no matter how much you want to hang on to it.

This new state of being brings new feelings. An urge I don't like. Is this what drove those poor creatures back in town? This feeling that I must devour the living or I'll burst open at the seams, explode into pieces?

It isn't safe, I think. *I'm not safe.*

I don't want to freak Jenny out, so I keep it to myself. If I can only hold on long enough to get her and E to the cabin. At least there they'll have a chance at staying safe and hidden. After that, I'll run as deep into these woods as I've ever been and lose myself somewhere so far from them, I'll never find my way back, no matter how much I want to.

And I will howl my true name to the trees.

A Bad Joke

A rook, a crow, and a raven strut into a bar.

"What's the clamor?" says the bartender, shooing the rook away with a dirty rag.

The minister smirks at the crow. "If I didn't know better, I'd think those there birds wanna murder us."

The priest pokes at the raven. "That would be awful unkind, wouldn't it?"

All three men laugh. Briefly.

Turtle and Owl

Turtle: This is all terribly interesting, isn't it?

Owl: You think so, do you-who-who?

Turtle: Definitely. Look at that one over there. What do you think it is?

Owl: Woodchuck

Turtle: Groundhog, I think

Owl: What's the difference?

Turtle: Dunno. Could be a muskrat

Owl: Or gopher. Too smushed to tell. Shall we ask it?

Turtle: Dunno. Looks busy. Maybe later

Owl: Marmot

Turtle: Pardon?

Owl: Marmot. That's another one it could be

Turtle: Not around here surely?

Owl: Could have traveled. Some creatures do get around, you know. Fast movers

Turtle: Is that a dig at me?

Owl: No. I mean, not really

Turtle: We're not as slow as reputed when we have some place we want to be

Owl: Not fast enough to stop getting your shell cracked to pieces

Turtle: Look who's talking. Last time I checked, most owls don't have only one leg and wing and don't have to rely on squatting on a broken-down turtle to get around

Owl: No need to rub it in

Turtle: Still, it is interesting, isn't it? Makes you think

Owl: About what?

Turtle: Life and death. What happens after. Do you think we'll go on and on like this?

Owl: Nah, we'll run out of humans soon

Turtle: Not that. I mean, do you think you and I will go on as we are forever? If we're already dead, we can't die but we can't go back to the way we were either. This isn't anything like what I thought the afterlife would be as I lay dying

Owl: I didn't have time to think. WHAP! And that was it. Luckier than you, I guess. Less pain. What did you think would happen next?

Turtle: We believe the Tortoise Spirit comes to collect us. We are gathered and buried in the Golden Sands like eggs and are reborn into a new shell

Owl: Huh. Must've been disappointing when this tortoise dude didn't show up. What's the difference between a tortoise and a turtle anyhow?

Turtle: I don't know. What's the difference between a frog and a toad?

Owl: Same as between a groundhog and a woodchuck maybe. Human names anyway. What do they know. Look what they've come to in the end. Nothing they don't deserve, of course. A cruel fate for cruel creatures

Turtle: Some of them are nice. More than once, I've had one stop and carry me across the road. Usually in the opposite direction to what I wanted to go, but it was a kind thought anyway

Owl: See what I mean? Why didn't they carry you in the direction you were going if they were determined to interfere? Cruelty comes natural to that lot. Exactly why we owls always ignore them

Turtle: I suppose you might have a point. Do owls have a theory about what happens after you die?

Owl: Why should anything happen? You fly, you hunt, you die. That's it. Or it should be. Pretty annoyed I'm still here, if I'm honest

Turtle: Yes, it's not as if we have much to offer to the fight

Owl: Though it was cool how you tripped that one up

Turtle: It was more by accident than anything, but it did give that flock of ducks a chance to give her a good going over

Owl: Nibbled to death by ducks, what a way to go

Turtle: Better than geese though

Owl: Absolutely. Geese are the worst

Turtle: You have to admit we've seen some amazing sights tonight. That has to count for something. We'll be able to say we were there, the night it all happened

Owl: I guess. If we're still around. At the rate I'm molting, won't be much left of me soon

Turtle: Yeah, I'm not feeling so hot myself. Maybe we'll get a chance to see the afterlife after all

Owl: That big tortoise coming for you?

Turtle: Wouldn't it be something? What's that?

Owl: What

Turtle: The golden light. Don't you see it?

Bear and Wolf and Fox

The bear stands watch at the southern end of town. Skirmishes are still flourishing here and there but the war is over for all intents and purposes. The dead now rule this place. He speculates whether the humans would have come back to life if enough of their bodies had been left intact. Is glad they left none in condition to test out the theory—there is no room in his new world order for Man. They have had their time. He thinks to call his army together. Congratulate them on a good night's work. Accept their accolades for the part he has played as their leader. He must plan his next steps, for this is only the beginning. He hugs his power and triumph to his broken self and does not hear another enemy at his back until it is too late.

The wolf has gathered his own troops from the long dead and newly turned. Has painted the bear as a fool, unfit to lead. He is no orator, but his words drip like sap from a wounded tree, sweet and sticky but so pleasant to consume. He has his own plans for the world that will be and his position in it. He was once leader of his pack and knows no other way to be. He was not designed to be a follower. As he drags his halved body forward, a host of horrors follow him, not yet tired of battle.

The fox observes from a safe distance. Sees the clash that will follow. She'll play no part, pick no side. Settles down comfortably to await the outcome while keeping an eye on the sky. No night lasts forever and this one is nearly over.

Human: Jenny

This is okay
it's okay
everything will be okay
we're okay...

The chant swamps my brain as we cross the last few hundred yards to the cabin. Cyrus leads the way, crashing through the forest like a mad thing, like time is running out on... something. I lift E onto my back, and he clasps his thin arms around my neck, nearly choking me. And none of this is okay and I know it but I'm trying not to think, just move. There'll be time to think about it later when we're all safe...

...but Cyrus isn't safe and never will be again, will he? He's dead dead dead

Hard to accept when I watch him striding ahead. He looks strong and vital and very much the person I have loved my whole life, yet with an air of confidence I've never seen before. I don't know what makes me more sad—that he's dead, or that it's only in death he's finally coming into his own.

Can't believe I never realized, never guessed. I thought I knew everything about him after our endless conversations—alright, arguments. About us, about coming out and going public, be damned to what the town thought. And in all that time, he never trusted me enough to confess his deepest secret, his hidden desire, his truest self.

I feel like a complete failure. Like I was never the friend I thought I was. I didn't hear the things left unsaid, hints I should have picked up on. Too wrapped up in my own vision of our future, a future he couldn't see, wasn't brave enough to pursue. Had to admit I'd looked down on him for that. Thought myself so superior for being willing to put everything out there, put ourselves on the line, even into physical danger, because there were plenty in town who weren't shy about acting out against anything they didn't like or understand in the ugliest of ways.

But it's okay, right? I know who he is and always wanted to be now and dawn will come, this night will end and there's the cabin finally and we'll be safe there and everything will be okay.

Roadkill

They've been here, pawed through my camp, stolen my food. I don't even know why I give a shit. What use is any of this crap to me now?

But it was mine. Everything I owned in the world except what I had on the night I got killed.

The blue tarp that kept the worst of the rain off *(the construction worker who blessed me out as I ran away with it)*. A couple of shirts and an extra pair of pants ripped from a clothesline *(that fucking huge dog that chased me)*. An old sleeping bag rescued from a dumpster *(the women who stood and sneered at me in disgust as I climbed out)*.

I kick through the pile of junk that was my home. When you got nothing, it's stupid, I guess, but the smallest things are important. Blue glass glints at me. A goblet I found in the trash. It has a chip out of the rim, so you gotta be careful when you drink, but it reminds me of a set my grandma had stored away in her fancy dish cabinet. Only brought out for special occasions. It's funny—I can't remember the last time we used them. Somebody's birthday, maybe, or an Easter dinner.

Christ! My memories are all fucked up. Everything's so far away, like a train chugging into a tunnel while I stand on the tracks and watch its lights fade. Wondering where it's going and why it wouldn't take me with it.

Always left behind. Always someone's punching bag. Always disrespected. Always powerless.

But not anymore. I got their scent. It's those same girls I been following. I'm gonna find them and take back what's mine.

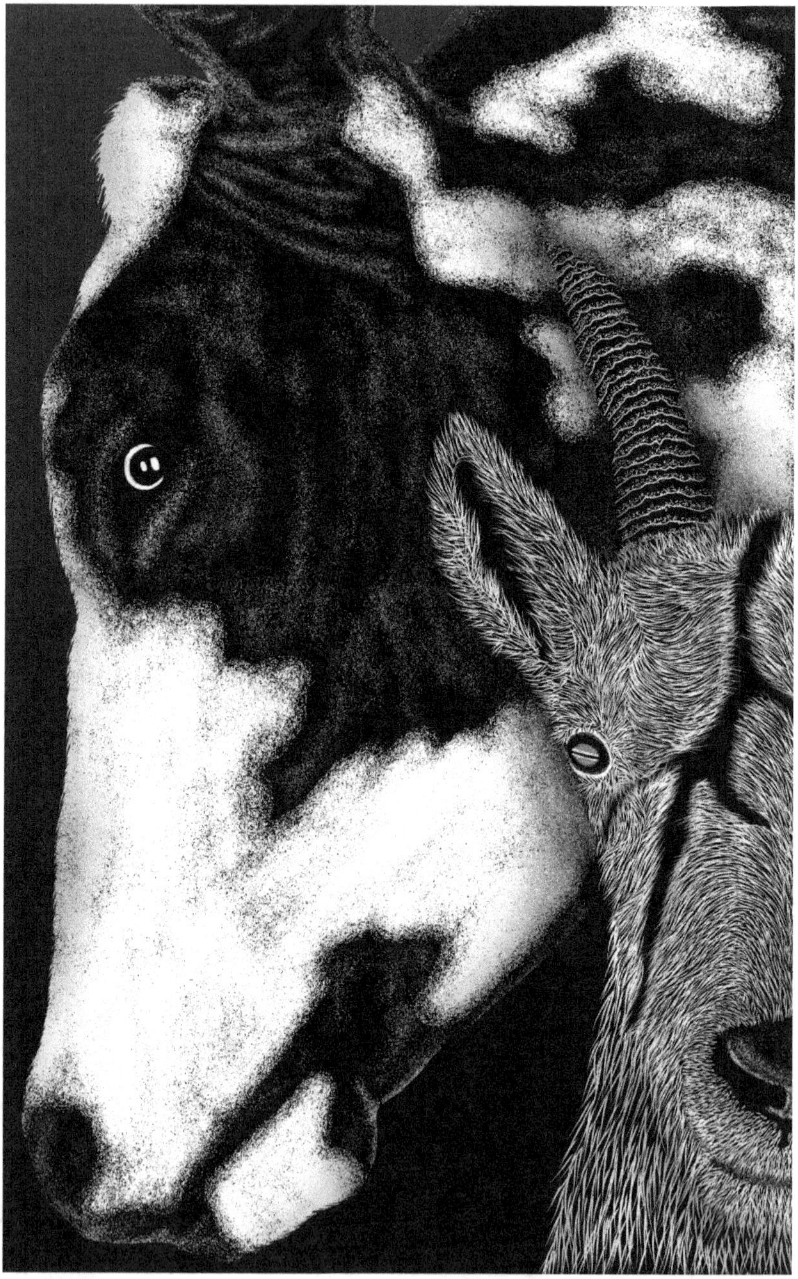

Cow and Goat

Whatzit?

I'm a goat. Whatta bout you?

Cow, innit.

What happened?

Gate open. Wandered out. Was fun for a bit. Got scared. Ran this way. Ran that way. Don't remember. You?

Jumped, didn't I? Never met another goat could jump as high as me. Fences ain't for shit if you can jump.

Fences are our friends. Fences keep us safe.

Fuck fences! Humans think they can keep us prisoners. Liberty and the open road for me.

Looks painful though.

So I lost a horn and an ear.

And an eye and a leg.

Yeah, yeah, so what? I jumped once and I'd do it again. Small price to pay for living free.

Don't think you're living.

But I am free. You can't argue with that. Ain't you glad to be free?

Miss the barn. Warm hay. Warm bodies. The sound of the others, huffing and puffing in the dark. Snorts. Moo moo MOO M O O O O O

Whoa, take it easy there, bud. Don't get yourself worked up. Your mind's been washed.

What?

I heard a human talking about it once. They washed all the shitty things about being a prisoner out of your brain, so you only remember the good stuff. You gotta be smarter than them.

I am not smart.

Who says?

The herd. The herd says I am not smart.

Well, they're wrong. They're just trying to hold you down.

Wash my brain?

Right! Besides, what if you ain't the brightest heifer in the herd? Don't mean nothing. Look at us now, smashing these humans to bits. Speaking of, shouldn't we get back to it?

They do make a nice squishy noise when you bounce up and down on them.

That's the spirit!

Human: Cyrus

The cabin is dark and cool and quiet. I light a couple of the old oil lanterns and take stock of the kitchenette. There's a ton of canned food and even some bottled water courtesy of Uncle Boomer's prepper obsession. We used to make fun of his paranoia but turns out he wasn't so far off. It's a relief to know that along with the stuff we picked up at the abandoned camp in the woods, there'll be enough at least for a couple of weeks or even more if Jenny's careful. It's good I'm dead when you look at it that way. One less mouth to feed.

There's a rifle and a shotgun and plenty of ammunition. I store the guns away on the highest shelf to keep them out of E's reach and bring in firewood in case Jenny needs to use the woodstove. She'll have to decide if it's worth the risk of attracting attention by lighting it. Smoke coming out the chimney would be a dead giveaway someone was here.

As I work, I notice my strength has become extraordinary. It's like being a god in a way or a superhero, but what a price to pay for it. I help Jenny sort out sheets for the camp beds and make sure the locks on the windows and doors are in working order, all the while thinking about how soon I can get away. I feel myself growing more and more detached, receding from being human toward what, I don't know, but I'm afraid whatever it is, it won't be fit to be around Jenny and E.

E found an old toy among the random trashy paperbacks and other junk that's piled up over the years. It's one of those handheld puzzles where you tilt it back and forth to try and get three little metal balls to line up in the holes. He seems both frustrated and fascinated.

He's a mess. Filthy, bloodstained. We should try to get him cleaned up, but he's content for the moment, so we leave him sitting on a cot, concentrating fiercely on the challenge while we walk outside to make a circuit of the cabin, making sure there's no obvious holes in the structure or undead animals lurking, ready to pounce.

It's so peaceful. Only the normal forest noises we're used to from spending time up here together every summer.

"I gotta go," I say.

She's already shaking her head "no" before I get the words out. "We need you. I need you. I can't do this alone."

"You're not alone. You got E. You're great with kids. They love you."

"It's not the same. I need you. Why can't you stay with me?"

"What would be the point? I'm dead, remember? Guts hanging out. Zombie eat brains," I joke, raising my hands out in front of me and lurching around. Okay, it's not a very good joke and Jenny agrees. The look she gives me is well-deserved.

"Don't," she says. Just that word. We stand and stare at each other a long minute.

"I'm sorry." I reach out and tuck strands of red hair that have come loose from her ponytail back behind her ears, brushing them gently from her face. She grabs my hand and kisses my palm.

"You're colder than you were," she whispers.

"Yeah."

"Do you... do you feel like those animals do—angry, I guess?"

"It's hard to describe. There's this pressure building up inside, like I'm gonna burst if something doesn't happen, if I don't do something. I don't know how long I can control it. If I wasn't already dead, it would kill me if I ever hurt you. I can't stay here. It's not safe. I need to put as much distance between us as I can before something happens."

"Fuck."

"Yeah, fuck." That gets a smile out of her. She always teases me about never cursing. I crush her in a bear hug.

"I love you, Cyrus," she mumbles into my shirt.

I lift her chin. "I love you, Jenny."

It's not our first kiss but in some way, it feels like it is. There's still enough of the human in me to enjoy the thrill of it. *Jenny loves me!* I want to shout to the whole world. *Me, Cyrus*!

But I have to go before I do anything that might change that.

"The sky looks better. More normal," she says. "Maybe things will settle down."

I'm about to agree when there's a commotion back the way we came to the cabin. Something's coming and it's big.

Fuck.

Wolf and Fox

The bear lay in pieces, broken beyond any hope of repair or resurrection. One solitary glassy eye looked reproachfully at the grey wolf amidst the carnage. The wolf sniffed it once, picked it up delicately with his front teeth and squashed it, enjoying the feel of the juices dribbling down his throat. Victory was never in doubt but still to be relished.

He raised his nose to the sky and howled, a shadow of his former call, it is true, but effective nonetheless. His army hooted and growled, honked and roared. Few of them understood the point of it all. Wolf or bear was just the same as long as the humans were gone, but it was still very pleasant to be on the winning side of any battle.

The wolf himself would be hard pressed to articulate what his victory meant, what next steps he planned to take. He only knew he must be the leader. It was his nature. At least, so he explained to the fox, although she had asked no questions but only wandered up after all was decided and cocked her head to one side.

"There can't be two alphas," Asha said. "It would be against the order of things."

"I see."

"I'll be a much better leader than the bear. He hadn't the imagination to envision creating an army as I have done."

“I see.”

“I suppose you think you could do better? Would you like to challenge me?”

“No, it’s not worth it.”

“It wouldn’t be, as you couldn’t hope to win such a fight.”

“I suppose, but that’s not what I mean. I only meant I believe your reign will be a short one. Have you noticed the sky? Dawn is coming and the storm is lowering. I think our time will be over soon. Life is best left to the living. Make the most of what you have remaining would be my advice. I know what I want to do with mine.”

So saying the fox turned and trotted away, disappearing into what yet lingered of the night.

Human: Jenny

He came out of nowhere. It's a man, but his head is all smashed in, shaped in a way it shouldn't be, one eye an empty hole. There are bits and pieces of him missing like he's been partially torn apart or pecked at by birds, and his clothes are rags. My first thought is he's another victim of the creatures, but then he screams at us.

"YOU STOLE MY STUFF. CAN'T EVEN RESPECT A DEAD MAN'S THINGS. I'M FUCKING SICK OF NOBODY GIVING ONE FLYING RAT'S ASS ABOUT ME!"

I'm backing up as fast as I can until I hit the wall of the cabin and can't go any farther, but Cyrus runs forward with a rage I would never have expected of him and tackles the guy, bringing them both down into the dirt. They struggle there in grimly determined silence except for a few grunts from time to time. The fury they feel radiates off them with a heat like the forest itself is on fire.

I hear a whimper and see E out of the corner of my eye. I'm shaking, but I force myself to walk over to him. "Go back inside, sweetie."

"What are they doing?"

"Just playing, E. Wrestling like on the TV."

"Like Cool Man Crawley?"

"Right."

"I wanna watch."

"Maybe later, E. They're practicing now. They'll put on a show later, okay?" I start dragging him away, but he's stubborn so I have to pick him up and haul him back inside. "You need to do what I say, E."

"Why? You're not my mama and my name's not E. It's Eddie."

"Well, Eddie starts with an E so we weren't so far off, were we? And your mama's not here but she'd want you to obey me. I'm taking care of you for her, you know, like babysitting. Didn't you ever have a babysitter before?"

"Sure, Pamela. She stinks."

He makes such a disgusted face that it's not so hard to fake a laugh. "I probably do too after the time we've had tonight." I kneel, hands on his shoulders. "Please, Eddie, it's really important you do what I say this once and stay here while I go back outside. I need to check on Cyrus. He's our friend, right?"

Eddie reaches out a hand and wipes the tears from my cheek. "Don't cry. I don't like it when Mama cries. I'll be good. And you can call me E."

"That's awesome, E. I'll be right back."

I run outside to find Cyrus and the man in a standoff, back on their feet and circling each other like bears before they charge. The woods are so quiet, like the trees are holding their breath in anticipation.

A golden ray of sunshine breaks through the treetops. Dawn at last. The ragged man steps into the sunspot and goes limp, like a puppet whose strings have been cut, falling in an awkward heap on the ground. He continues to make jerky little movements and moan but shows no signs of getting up again.

Cyrus is huffing and puffing as I approach and turns on me with a growl that freezes me. He looks like a stranger until his eyes soften up and he grins. "What if we're not zombies but vampires? Looks like we might be allergic to sunlight."

"Come away inside," I hiss, knowing with every fiber of my being he won't.

He shakes his head and smiles and I'm about to lose him a second time and there's nothing I can do to stop it.

Vulture

What a night it's been. Exhilarating! The sights, the sounds, the stench. It's been grand. I'm glad I became one of them and played my part, but for the first time since my death, I find myself growing weary. The storm overhead has died down. The green sky is lightening, and for the only moment in my life or death, I fear the coming of the sun.

A notion strikes me. Sentimental, perhaps, but now the battle is won, I will seek out the place where Nyx lies and see if any part of her is there still. She died so long ago, devoured by beetle and worm, scattered by the little creatures that gnaw and tear at the dead. There wouldn't have been enough of her left to join our party. But if I can find even one small bone or ebon feather that still retains her essence, I will lay myself down beside it and rest awhile.

Human: Jenny

Cyrus steps forward until he's standing in the sun with the same smile on his face and his eyes locked with mine. As the golden light hits him, he slams onto his back on the ground like a felled tree.

"Cyrus, what have you done," I moan, kneeling beside him.

"Put an end to it, I hope. I feel it fading, whatever it was that kept us going. Don't be sad. I didn't want to live that way, if you can call it living." His voice is growing hoarse like it's hard to talk. "But I'm glad I got to tell you my name. Do me a favor if you can?"

"Of course."

"If there's any scissors or a razor in the cabin, give me a buzzcut? I always wanted one but was too afraid to do it. Why don't you go look?"

"In a minute. I don't want to leave you."

"I'm not going anywhere. Go on, Jenny, love. For me."

I'm barely aware of getting to my feet and running to the cabin. I root frantically through the bathroom drawers while E watches me wide-eyed. I find some scissors, rusty and dull, but they'll have to do. I'm not gone more than a minute, but it's too long.

He's motionless in the sunlight, eyes closed with a smile lingering on his face. A fly buzzes, landing on his bloodied shirt. I shoo it away in horror. Weep and cut. Stop from time to time to wipe my eyes so I can see, then weep and cut some more. The black curls fall to the ground and start to waft away on the morning breeze. It's a hack job, but I neaten it up the best I can. Save a few curls for myself and leave the rest for any birds still among the living to line their nests for winter.

I get the ragged man up into an old wheelbarrow with partially flat tire and take him off deep into the woods to dump. I guess I should feel sorrier about abandoning him, but I only have so much energy and strength and I'll need it for the task ahead.

Six feet down doesn't sound like much until you try to dig through root and rock. I have to abandon two holes before I finally find a place soft enough to dig deep. It's noon by the time I get it done, so I take a break to make lunch for me and E. He's quiet and well-behaved—too polite even, like he gets the gravity of what I've been working on and doesn't want to be a bother to me. He's gonna have to grow up way too fast, but maybe he at least has a chance now.

I wrap Cyrus in one of my grandmother's quilts that I'd always loved, a Jacob's ladder pattern of clear blues and greens, faded and mellowed with long aging. Tie him up with some cord wound round and round like a package and wheel him out to the hole. There's no elegant way to get him in so I lay him out along the edge and roll him over as gently as I can.

Don't think I'll ever forget the awful *thunk* when he hits bottom. I recite the Twenty-third Psalm as I shovel dirt into the hole. It's the only Bible verse I ever learned by heart, and it seems as good as any to recite even if I don't believe the words. It would feel wrong not to say something.

Cyrus would have laughed at me, but I don't think he'd mind if he knew it gives me some comfort.

I pat down the dirt with the shovel as hard as I can. I'll get E to help me gather some rocks and small stones to place on top when I've recovered my strength. I don't want some animal digging him up. He deserves an undisturbed rest. Deserved so much more than that. I lie down beside the grave and watch the trees swaying in the sun against a cloudless blue sky. Whisper a heartfelt "Fuck you" to the universe.

Fox

The fox trots away from the wolf and what's left of the bear. Away from the town and the horrors within. Past the little country houses which hold their own cryptic secrets now. She keeps to the shadows and the shade. Has witnessed more than one of the undead dropping in the sunlight and senses her end is near, but there is one more task ahead. She waits until night falls again to cross the wide road which offers no shelter from the sky.

She slinks through the forest, down well-remembered paths. Is cautious of the cabin—sees a human who has escaped the culling, senses its sorrow. If it has been spared, who is she to put an end to it? Perhaps its suffering will be the worse for having to go on alone, for there is intense grief in loneliness. As she watches though, a small one comes to the human, puts its arms around her, and they rock together, mother and child, in the moonlight.

This reminds her of her own errand. Time grows short. Even now, in the return of darkness, she feels weaker than before. She finds the spot she wants, a shallow groove in the earth under a bush which has shed most of its leaves to the autumn winds. It's far enough away that she hopes she will not be a worry to them, but close enough to observe them one last time.

Dawn comes again. They venture out, her two kits, brothers. She is pleased to see them looking so well. They were barely weaned when she was killed. Too young to be left on their own, but they have not only survived but thrived. They are older and more serious but haven't totally lost their childish ways. They romp and roll, wrestling and nipping at each other in jest.

Their mother watches and smiles as the morning sunlight seeks out the weak spots in her shelter, filtering in to warm her cold, cold bones. As she slowly fades away under its gentle influence, her final thought is, "They are safe."

An Inventory (of the Dead by the Living)

As the sun climbs higher, we gather to pay homage to the dead. To mark each spot where this one or that one has fallen. To wonder at their stories and speculate on what heroic deeds they performed on the Night of All Nights.

A grey wolf lies at the center of an immense army. One at least of every creature we have ever seen or heard tell of. The wolf is a pitiable sight. Its back half is nowhere to be seen. What courage, what determination it must have taken to drag this ravaged body into battle. No wonder these others were drawn to it, an honor guard for what must have been a brave, a selfless, a noble soul. We bow in reverence.

Farther afield we notice two does, so alike they must be twins. They lie, necks entwined while others of their herd are nestled here and there among the tall grass close by. How graceful they are, even at rest. And what is this? The mere skeleton of a possum cradles a hare's head in its boney hands, nose pressed to nose as though they were in deep conversation or communion at the moment of cessation. A strange pair but hardly the most unlikely we observe.

The chipmunk and alligator? Some among us laugh gently but kindly to see these companions, so mismatched in size and temperament, but others weep in pity at the poor things, such feeble mockeries of their former selves. A pond full of koi is a livelier scene. The gold and orange beauties nibble on a spotted silver-scaled carcass floating along the surface. To provide sustenance to others, to be of service even in this most final of deaths. What a satisfying end it must be.

We stop to smooth and rearrange the ruffled feathers of a fat turkey. Our heroes deserve every attention, every final dignity we can grant them. A splendid creature! Not even the ruinous shape of his head can mar his magnificence when order is restored to his form. This owl is not as fortunate. Such a proud hunter in life—so disfigured now, but its remaining wing drapes over the broken shell of a turtle of impressive size. The turtle has such a contented look upon its face. As if its last thoughts were filled with both light and delight.

Alongside the river, we find an earthen dam reinforced with bone. It is a magnificent feat of building, and we linger to admire it and the beaver couple, frozen together forever in a last embrace much as the pair of mourning doves discovered breast to breast on a low branch. Any fate can be made palatable, can be endured with grace when one loves and is loved in return.

A cow and a goat are the only farm animals our group comes across. Some among us used to envy these tamed souls, kept secure from the harms of the wider world with food aplenty, but the wisest of us believe there was no safety from Man, whether as a domesticated creature or one as wild as these feral piglets nestled lovingly at their mother's belly. Such is the corruption of Man that it touches every one of us, soon or late. Our world will survive and thrive without their blight.

And thus is our day spent. It is not near long enough for us to visit all the fallen, and some portion of our party drift away at each new discovery. Perhaps the sorrow of marking the dead becomes too much, or perhaps they wish to forget, to move on, to live, as is their right. Those of us who remain on patrol believe each of these soldiers deserves a final benediction, acknowledgement of their sacrifice, so we do not rest until we have visited as many as we can.

There are not a few of us who regret we were ineligible to take part in the great campaign because we still draw breath. What feats shall we ever perform in our common, everyday lives to compare with the glory that has unfolded here? With what renown will we be endowed? Dedicated and sincere mourners are we, but in the end, observers only. Survivors. The living.

Then again, if none were left alive to remember the dead, their fame and the dreadful price they paid for it would also disappear, be forgotten. That must not be. We will share our memories and keep their stories alive in our generation and the generations yet to be born into this new realm, so savagely bought, so fiercely made.

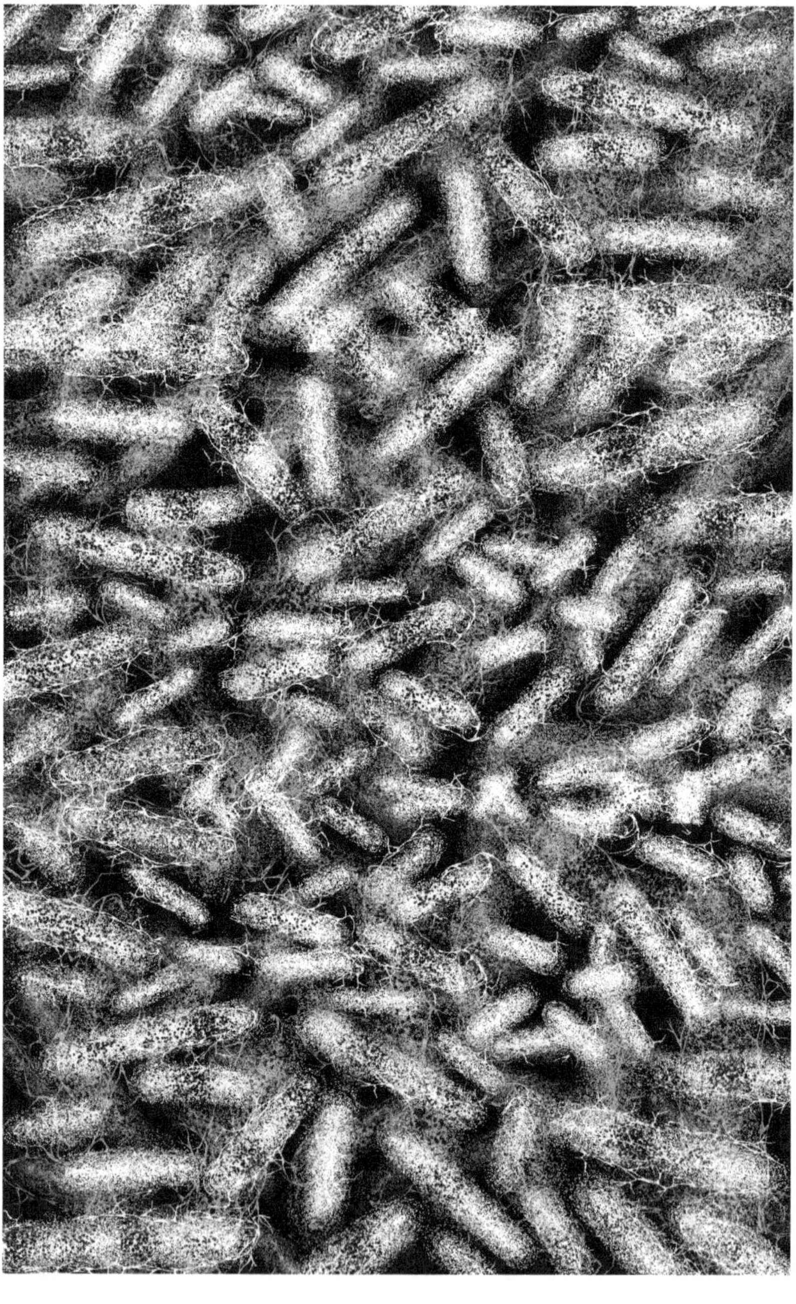

Bacteria

there are
so many
of these things
everywhere

a most generous spread

they shuddered
crawled
fell where they lay
so nasty
so tasty

a novel treat
we must eat our fill
so we can

S

P

L

I

T

& multiply & multiply & multiply & multiply
& multiply & multiply & multiply & multiply
& multiply & multiply & multiply & multiply
& multiply & multiply & multiply & multiply
& multiply & multiply & multiply & multiply
& multiply & multiply & multiply & multiply
& multiply & multiply & multiply & multiply
& multiply & multiply & multiply & multiply
& multiply & multiply & multiply & multiply
& multiply & multiply & multiply & multiply
& multiply & multiply & multiply & multiply
& multiply & multiply & multiply & multiply
& multiply & multiply & multiply & multiply
& multiply & multiply & multiply & multiply
& multiply & multiply & multiply & multiply
& multiply & multiply & multiply & multiply
& multiply & multiply & multiply & multiply
& multiply & multiply & multiply & multiply
& multiply & multiply & multiply & multiply
& multiply & multiply & multiply & multiply
& multiply & multiply & multiply & multiply
& multiply & multiply & multiply & multiply
& multiply & multiply & multiply & multiply
& multiply & multiply & multiply & multiply
& multiply & multiply & multiply & multiply
& multiply & multiply & multiply & multiply
& multiply & multiply & multiply & multiply
& multiply & multiply & multiply & multiply
& multiply & multiply & multiply & multiply
& multiply & multiply & multiply & multiply

Epitaph for Humans by Members of the Family Corvidae

(A short scene)

Setting: an overgrown human cemetery as dawn approaches

Cast of characters: Stu, a crow; Frank, a rook; Manny, a raven; and a magpie named Maggie

"There's nothing more ominous than an omen, Frank," the magpie said.

"I don't know, Maggie. Portents are pretty powerful. What d'you think, Stu? Portent or omen?"

"Me, personally?" said the crow. "I always wanted to be a harbinger of doom, a-tip-tapping on a window at midnight. That's gotta be the pinnacle, right?"

"What are you lot going on about?" Manny complained. He was older and wiser than the rest, with little patience for their idle chatter.

"Thinking about back in the Before Times," Frank replied. "When there was humans about. Those ijits was so easy to fright. Remember the time a bunch of us gathered on the high wire in town and just stared at 'em for an hour without moving?"

Stu cackled. "Their stoopid faces! That was a hoot and a half, weren't it?"

Manny sniffed. "Until one of them pulled out a pistol and killed poor Claude. None of you were laughing then."

"Claude always was a dreamer. Too wrapped up in his own thoughts. The rest of us heard your warning right enough and got out of there before death flew."

"You young ones always were too bold and disrespectful. Humans were our biggest enemy and threat, yet you treated them like a joke."

"And so they was," Frank said. "Afraid of a bunch of birds. Besides, they got served up their own kind of justice in the end, didn't they? All gone. Every one of them."

"Yeah! We got the last laugh," Stu said. "'A murder of crows' they called my kind. And Maggie and hers 'a mischief of magpies!' They didn't know we called them 'a foolishness of ijits,' did they?"

"Foolishness was right," Frank agreed with satisfaction. "The Great Armies took care of them, didn't they? We ain't never been better off in our lives than now. No more smoke, no more noise. The good green world righting itself more and more each day. Never been so much of every kind of food running around for us to snatch. And you notice how it tastes different? Pure and clean. Good riddance, ain't that right, Maggie?"

"You've been quiet, Maggie," Manny observed. "Don't you agree with these two?"

The magpie rustled her wings uneasily. "It's true the air is sweeter and we've less to fear, but—"

"But what?" Stu croaked. "These is the best times to be alive, Maggie. Ain't you glad you lived to see it?"

"I suppose."

Manny draped one wing around the magpie. "What is it, child? What worries you?"

"There was a human I used to visit. A female with hair as bright as a cardinal's feathers. She gave me shiny things to decorate my nest and saved me tidbits from her dinner. Talked to me of her life. It was a sad tale. She lost her mate on the Night of All Nights and then her chick from the illness that took off any who survived the War. But before she got too sick herself, I'd repeat words back to her, and it dimpled her face with a smile I liked to see. Tickled to have someone to talk with, I think. She was alone at the end. I flew in an open window and perched by her bed. She was so glad to see me. Sang me a song, a song of their long ago as her breath faded.

I remember it still:

There were three ravens sat in a tree
And they were black as they might be
The one of them said to his mate:
'What shall we for our breakfast take?'"

"Breakfast?" squawked Frank. "Now you're talking my language! C'mon, Stu. That old church in town has a healthy bustle of fat beetles at work in the steeple."

The rook and crow flew off in a rush of wings with nary a look behind them.

"Don't mind those two, Maggie," the raven said. "The young are always thoughtless and foolish. They don't remember as much of the Before Times as they should."

“I hope you don’t think I’m foolish too, feeling sorry for a human?”

Manny was silent a moment, staring off into the lightening sky before speaking.

“There was an old, old human once. Sat in the park every day. He’d perch his soft hat on his knee and spread seed on the ground. He was lonely, too, I believe, for he would speak to us gathered there like we were one of his own kind. I was young then and greedy, too busy feasting to pay much attention. But I remember one day, I looked up and caught him watching me. His eyes were... well, they were warm and soft, and he gave me a nod, like one bird to another. An acknowledgment as it were. It gave me a strange feeling. As though if he were a raven, or I was a human, we might have been friends.”

“Could you not be friends as it was?”

“Humans were always our enemies, Maggie. You should never forget that. The behavior of one or two cannot make up for it. But still...”

Maggie spoke softly into the silence that followed. “It is a memory of kindness, for both of us. I think they would like to be remembered, if only while we live. In a few generations, all remembrance of the Before Times will be gone. Maybe we should tell the children so they may tell theirs. Of the human with the bright hair...”

“...and the one with the soft hat? You should make up a song, Maggie. You’ve a pretty voice. And we will pass it down.”

“A song of our long ago?”

“Yes, such as it will be soon.”

Maggie closed her eyes, thinking hard, before singing softly:

There was a human with bright, bright hair
And one with warmth in his eyes
They saw us birds for what we were
And never told us lies

"Very nice, Maggie. Very nice indeed. Sing it again for me and again. I will learn it too so we can teach the others."

And so they did.

THE END

About the Author

Helen Whistberry (she/they) is the pen name for an indie author and artist who began writing after retiring from a long career working in libraries. They have published numerous books as well as contributing horror and fantasy stories to anthologies. Helen's writing often explores their own experiences with gender, asexuality, alienation, and autism. Their whimsical digital artwork focuses on the natural world. Helen also loves to read and review books by fellow indie and small press authors. You can find out more by visiting their website for a complete list of publications and links: https://www.helenwhistberry.com/

I hope you enjoyed this tale. If you have the time and inclination, reviews left on any of the major review sites are always greatly appreciated. Thank you so much for your support and for accompanying me on this writing and art journey.

Sign up for my newsletter to keep up to date with all my doings and receive a free ebook of my forest stories, The Melody of Trees! Link: https://BookHip.com/QVZXZGM

What would you do if you were shipwrecked, swept ashore, and menaced by a horde of ravenous crabs, only to be saved by an eldritch being and welcomed into a tower of secrets by an even more enigmatic host? As a scientist and traveler, how would you assess a situation that could only be a nightmare such as no human has ever experienced?

Join Avery Mothmere on the adventure of a lifetime! This charming story is by turns Gothic horror, strange romance, unfathomable mystery, and weird fever dream. **Features 30 original illustrations by the author.** Link: https://books2read.com/AveryMothmere

A lonely man shunned by society and haunted by a beautiful corpse. Sentient toys in a life and death struggle with unspeakable evil. Spectral visitations at midnight and in broad daylight. Fairy and folk tale re-imaginings full of eldritch places and events. Glimpses of the future and reminiscences of times past and times that never were and never will be. This generous selection of short stories encompasses genres from folk horror to dystopian sci fi, animal fantasy to ghost tales. Enter the imagination of Helen Whistberry and enjoy 19 unforgettable stories with the author's signature mix of horror and hope. Includes 20 original illustrations by the author. Link: https://books2read.com/ABrokenThing

Amelia Arrowheart is a homebody. Beatrice Buttons most decidedly is not. When these two ladies of a certain age meet and become fast friends, neither expects the extraordinary challenges they will face together and apart. Welcome to Lichen, a place like no other, where fungi are revered, cloud creatures crowd the skies, and sea witches wield their power for the good of all. Two mischievous little boys, a space pirate, and a monster that reaches out from the depths of the ocean will change their lives forever. Join Beatrice and Amelia on the adventure of a lifetime as they take to the skies and plunge into the depths of the sea to save a friend and break a curse! A unique and uplifting fantasy tale celebrating friendship, loyalty, and love. Includes 33 original illustrations! Link: https://books2read.com/WaveOfWitches

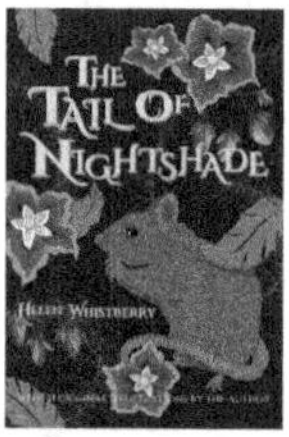

"A mouse scrabbled along under crisp, fallen leaves, whiskers twitching. Death, disguised as an owl, kept watch high above, unblinking eyes orbed bright in the moonlight..." Thus begins an adventure unlike any other for Nightshade, a young mouse who never expected to venture very far from their cozy burrow. Over the course of a few eventful days, they will meet strangers both weird and magnificent, including an impetuous bear and a lovely wyrm, a flitter-flutter and a whirligig, a wizard of modest talents and a legendarily monstrous cat, and a most wondrous being of light. Together they will navigate a noble quest, face unimaginable dangers, and experience astonishing events. Through it all, they will cling to the one thing they most believe: there is no obstacle that cannot be overcome if all remain true. Includes 31 original illustrations by the author. Link: https://books2read.com/TailOfNightshade

Experience the unforgettable magic of these original stories and illustrations. You'll discover an elder god keeping a loving eye on their forest, a girl made of glass and other characters fighting for their lives against both impossible odds and monsters (human and otherwise), some wise guys having a supernaturally bad day, and the exploits of a loner gun-for-hire and his loyal dragon. From fantasy and folklore to horror and sci-fi, these tales are tied together not only by their forest settings but by a sense of humanity (even in those characters who aren't quite human), empathy for all creatures, and the weird beauty to be found in moments both light and dark. Each story accompanied by an original illustration by the author. Link: https://books2read.com/MelodyOfTrees

Mystery series set in mid-America in the 1950s. Light noir with a cozy mystery feel and a touch of the paranormal that pays loving tribute to the wise guy detectives of the 40s and 50s. Jim Malhaven is a goodhearted but down on his luck reporter at a small-time newspaper. He often gets more than he bargains for when his editor shoots him some unusual assignments and as much as he tries to avoid the supernatural, it seems intent on tracking him down! The Malhaven Mysteries are meant to be lighthearted and humorous while still acknowledging the realities of the period and place it is set in. Some violence that is on the milder side compared to most modern day thrillers and no harsh language. Find the first in the series here: https://books2read.com/WeirdSisters

www.ingramcontent.com/pod-product-compliance
Lightning Source LLC
Chambersburg PA
CBHW060457300726
48975CB00008B/2538
* 9 7 8 1 9 6 0 6 7 1 1 8 9 *